CALL OF THE WILD

Rebecca Caldwell concealed a secret, satisfied smile. Although her white warrior companion had done his best to sneak up on the camp and thus get one over on her, she had not been taken by surprise.

"I have quite a lot of bad news for you," he began.

"What is it, Lone Wolf? Are Tulley and Uncle Ezekial in Grub Stake?"

"That they are. You were right about Tulley rebuilding his gang. They're all there, close to thirty of the worst scum on the frontier. They are murdering miners, jumping claims, robbing others and generally terrorizing the town. Most people seem afraid of Tulley's men and I don't blame them. That many guns is a lot for peaceable people to face. They need help."

"Our kind of help?" Rebecca asked anxiously.

Lone Wolf thought a moment. "More like a U.S. Marshal and a posse—or troops. . . .

THE HOTTEST SERIES IN THE WEST CONTINUES!

WHITE SQUAW
#2
BOOMTOWN BUST
BY E. J. HUNTER

ZEBRA BOOKS
KENSINGTON PUBLISHING CORP.

ZEBRA BOOKS

are published by

KENSINGTON PUBLISHING CORP.
475 Park Avenue South
New York, N.Y. 10016

First printing: November, 1983

Printed in the United States of America

them with the fondness a warrior has for those who have ridden into battle beside him.

"Doc Silver says Matt is going to pull through," Mike offered as a last inducement for Rebecca to stay behind in Grub Stake.

"Yes. I saw him for a little while. The doctor says he probably won't regain consciousness before tomorrow. Tell him . . . tell him good-bye for me."

Already Lone Wolf had turned his pony's head toward the trail taken by the fleeing gang. Rebecca glanced at him, then looked back on the grateful people of Grub Stake. She lifted Ike's reins and turned the big sorrel's head.

"Good-bye to all of you. You are brave and kind and I thank you for all your help. Next time we corner the Tulley gang I'll have my final revenge."

Back straight, face radiant in the midday sun, the fringes of her white doeskin dress fluttering in the breeze, Rebecca Caldwell rode out of town on her ongoing quest for vengeance.

ONE

Bullets splintered wood from the bed of the buckboard wagonbox. The hot lead had first pierced the frail body of a young Indian boy. The corpse jumped with each impact. Sprawled across the spring-mounted seat lay the dead lad's mother and father, grotesque in the ugly postures of their demise. Another shot sounded and the youngster's body jerked violently.

"Damn' Injuns!" Bobby O'Toole yelled from astride his swaybacked mount. "Goddamned Injuns is the cause of it all. If you hadn't come by the Caldwell place that time and tooken off Rebeccey an' her Maw. If you hadda worked her to death like you should, 'stead o' lettin' her get away and come after us, why . . . why we wouldn't have to be robbin' reservation blanket Injuns to git money for our eats." The grossly fat, three-hundred-pound outlaw pumped his last bullet into the dead child.

"That's enough, Bobby," Clyde Morton complained. "We've gotta catch up to Jake and the rest. They're expectin' us in Chappel before the day's out."

"Oh, hell," the pooched-lipped bandit countered. "Them boys can look out for themselves. 'Sides, what we got to do once we get to Chappel. It ain't no bigger than a pimple on a bull's butt. What we need is a right nice sized little town with a big ol' bank, just bulgin' with money for us to take from it. Now, that's

5

style. That's the way the Bitter Creek Jake Tulley gang used to do things," O'Toole went on, remembering happier times.

"Then why ain't we doin' it like that now?" Morton, a newcomer inquired.

Bobby O'Toole gave him a dark look that terminated any further conversation along this line and began stripping the loot from the dead Sioux, mostly quarters, nickels and pennies.

The truth was that things had not gone well for the Bitter Creek Jake Tulley gang for the past thirty days. Five years ago the bandit crew had given Rebecca Caldwell and her mother, Hannah, to Iron Calf's Oglala in a deal to save their own worthless lives. The fourteen-year-old girl had survived the rigors of life as a slave to the Sioux and managed, at last, to escape.

She came hunting Jake Tulley and the men who had betrayed her, including her two low-life uncles, Ezekial and Virgil. She sought revenge. During the past month, she had exacted quite a lot of that. In the process she foiled the scheme of the gang's true mentor, Roger Styles. The ambitious and twisted young man had a plan whereby he and certain close associates would end up owning virtually all of the Dakota Territory. Of course the Sioux and Cheyenne would have to be moved out . . . or exterminated. This stumbling block gave Styles and his chief enforcer, Jake Tulley, little difficulty.

Tulley and his gang began selling rifles, ammunition and whiskey to the Sioux. Once the bucks got fired up, they reasoned, an uprising would be bound to occur. That would bring in the army to sweep the rolling plains free of the red savages, thus opening the way for Styles' ambitions. Tulley and his boys would be rewarded with what seemed an unlimited buffalo herd to decimate for the much coveted hides while Styles went on to become enormously rich on land deals, gold mining in the Black Hills and eventual political power in what would have to eventually become one or more new states in the Union.

Then Rebecca Caldwell began killing off the gang.

She, and her companion, Lone Wolf, himself a former White captive of the Crow, struck again and again at Jake Tulley's outlaw horde until, reeling under the cataclysmic power of a buffalo stampede and the bullets of the vengeance-minded girl and her sidekick, they fled Nebraska's east-central regions for less hostile environs.

Relentlessly, Rebecca and Lone Wolf still pursued them. Knowledge of this burned in the mind and soured the belly of Bitter Creek Jake Tulley while he sat at a green baize table in the only saloon in Chappel, Deuel County, Nebraska and gazed forlornly at the unpromising cards that lay before him.

"A dollar on the pair of treys," a young cowboy sitting across from Tulley announced. He flipped a cartwheel into the pot and grinned at the three men he considered his real adversaries in the poker game.

"I'll see that," Ezekial Caldwell offered while he tossed in his bet.

"By me," Tulley grumbled, folding his hand. "Not even a promising hole card."

"A dollar and up a dollar," Luke Wellington spoke in a near-whisper. The tall, lanky, cold-eyed gunhawk could almost be called handsome, except for the curving white scar that disfigured the left side of his face from eye socket to lip corner.

"I'll stay," a second wrangler put in mildly.

Up for a few days' toot from the ranch where they

7

worked, across the line in Colorado Territory, the two cowhands had unwittingly entered the game with the three least desirable men in the area of several states. Through most of the card play, Fate had smiled on the innocent pair. But then, she often raised high those whom she would destroy. The cards went around again.

An ace dropped on the green-clad table in front of the opener. "Thank ya, Wade," he told his partner, who had the deal.

Ezekial received his third visible diamond.

Luke Wellington paired up with his hole card.

Wade, the other cowboy, took an eight that helped his building straight.

"Two dollars on the bullet," the opener declared.

"Take it easy, Link," Wade told him good-naturedly. "You don't want to scare the rest of us out."

"You pair up with your hole card, Sonny?" Ezekial growled suspiciously. Always a poor loser, Ezekial Caldwell had encountered an exceptionally bad run of luck so far. He gloomily watched his stack of silver cartwheels and five and ten dollar gold pieces dwindle at an alarming rate.

"Maybe I did and maybe I didn't, Mister," Link replied cockily. "It'll only cost you two dollars to find out."

A grunt accompanied the clink of two more of Ezekial's silver hoard.

"Stay," Luke Wellington offered without hesitation.

Wade also remained around for the final card.

Link got his ace. Ezekial's scowl turned to a secretive glint of greed with a fourth diamond dropped before him. Luke Wellington licked dry lips when he stared down at a trash card. Wade filled the gaping center of his straight with a six and laid the

8

spent deck on the table.

"Five dollars," Link challenged.

"Two pair," Ezekial observed. "I'll call it, 'cause this time I know you're bluffing." A small gold coin clinked on the pile at the center of the table.

"Fold. I've donated enough this time around," Luke informed the players.

"Your five and I'll raise you five," Wade called out cheerily.

"A straight don't beat a flush, Kid," Ezekial taunted. "You'd a' been wise to fold along with Luke."

"I'll see your five," Link interrupted.

"Up that five more," Ezekial pressed. "I've got you boys this time." He glanced down at the four red-spotted cards that showed before him, then thumbed up the corner of his hole ducket. It mocked him, black as a moonless night.

The betting went around, both cowboys staying.

Ezekial had lost his bluff and the bitter knowledge of it set acid to eating at his stomach.

"Full house," Link gleefully announced. "Aces over treys." He reached out for the pile of coins. Ezekial's large, hairy paw fell over Link's hand.

"Hold on there. You boys seem to win all too often and much too easily."

"What is it you're proddin' at, Mister? C'mon, spit it out!" Link demanded in an angry voice.

"Are you callin' my pard a cheat?" Wade snarled. Then the import of Ezekial's words struck him. "You callin' us both cheaters?"

"As the old saying goes, 'If the shoe fits . . .'" Ezekial let it hang, though he clamped Link's wrist in iron-hard fingers.

"Mister, we've never cheated at anything. Take your hand off Link and . . . I think you owe us an apology." Wade's cold, commanding voice would have

9

sounded right coming from Jake Tulley.

"Better back down, boy," the outlaw leader advised. "You're askin' to buy into trouble like you never want to see. Either that . . . or fill your hand!"

Wade didn't make a move toward the short-barreled Colt Frontier model that he had tucked in his waistband.

All the same, Luke Wellington's Remington spoke with a stentorian voice and a billow of powder smoke concealed the stunned young cowhand from his murderer for a long moment.

Blood welled up behind Wade's tightly compressed lips. He wavered on his feet, eyes wide with shock and surprise, and slowly his muscles relaxed, devoid of conscious control. A scarlet ribbon unrolled from his sagging mouth and spread on his shirt. A soulful, bass groan escaped from deep in his chest and he toppled sideways out of his chair.

"You killed him, you bastard!" Link screamed. His free left hand streaked to his waist, where he kept an old Star revolver as proof against snakes.

Link never made it. Luke's big Remington bucked once more in his hard fist and the slug sizzled through the air.

It struck Link in the breastbone and sent a shower of bone chips into his lungs. Luke eared back the hammer once again and squeezed off another round that punched a hole an inch below the pocket button on Link's Palmer flannel trade shirt. The mortally wounded cowhand went over backwards to fall beside his dead friend.

"You've got a keen eye, Luke," Jake Tulley praised.

"Never lost it, Jake."

"You . . . Why, you murdered those boys in cold blood!" the agitated barkeep shouted. "This is . . . it's awful. What with no lawman in town . . ."

10

"Shut up, Hank," Luke Wellington interrupted. "And bring us another bottle. Killin' makes me thirsty. Or . . . do you want to wind up down there with these two wranglers?"

"Yessir, Mr. Wellington," Hank cringed. "Right away, sir."

"Send someone to do something about these two," Jake Tulley added. "We don't want them stinkin' up our game."

"Thanks, Luke," Ezekial Caldwell offered in a quiet voice. "I appreciate that. Those two were cheatin', I know it."

"Might be so. Only how could they out-cheat you, Zeke?"

Caldwell glowered at Luke and began to pick up the money scattered on the table. Outside, horses clopped up to the tie-rail and boots clomped on the narrow boardwalk. Bobby O'Toole and Clyde Morton entered the saloon.

"What's up?" O'Toole inquired. "We heard shootin'."

"Luke plugged a couple of range riders. They got uppity about bein' accused of cheatin'," Tulley told them. "You took your time getting here."

"We stopped to relieve some blanket Injuns of a little cash money," O'Toole explained.

"They happen to have a pretty young daughter?" Tulley asked shrewdly, well aware of O'Toole's disgusting sex practices. His hard, gray eyes fixed on the blubbery bandit.

"Naw. Only a little brat kid. An' then the feisty li'l fucker tried to bite me when I went to poke him in the rear. So I filled him fulla holes."

"O'Toole, you could gag a maggot!" Luke Wellington roared. "C'mon over and have a drink. Ain't nothin' else to do around here."

11

"Stage is in!" a voice called from the street, followed by the rattle of high, steel-rimmed wheels and the neighs of tired, hard-driven horses.

Ten minutes later, the Overland station operator, who also served Chappel as postmaster, strode into the saloon. In his hand he held a grease-smeared tan envelope and several wanted posters. He waved the sealed packet.

"Letter here for a Mister J. Tulley. Are you him?" he inquired of the assemblage around the deal table.

"I be," Jake Tulley answered up. He took the envelope and tore it open with a thick, callused forefinger. "Here, Luke read it aloud to me. It looks important."

"Why, Jake, I thought you could read. You play cards," Luke remarked while he took the letter and examined it.

"I know my numbers up to fifty," Tulley returned defensively. "An' I can make my signature an' read most of the big print words on a wanted flyer. That's enough of that sissy stuff for any man, ain't it?"

"Ain't no sissy stuff to be able to read, Jake," Luke protested, proud of his schooling, that extended through the seventh grade. "Ever'body ought to know how. Aah! This is from Roger Styles. He says, 'Dear Jake, I hope this finds you in good health and well away from that Caldwell bitch. When you receive this mis-missive'—whatever that means—'you must act immediately. Gather up the largest number of men you can and ride at once for Grub Stake, a new mining boomtown that has opened up here in Colorado Territory. It is vital that you act quickly. There is talk of statehood for Colorado, perhaps as soon as a year hence. If your gang can securely hold Grub Stake until after the territory becomes a state, it will insure that I can go to the state legislature as a

12

representative from that area.' " Luke stopped reading. "Well, can you beat that. Ol' Roger still wants to go into politics."

"Why not?" Tulley fired back. "That's where the big money is to be made. All that graft and under the table deals that's all the time talked about. An' you don't do nothin' to earn your pay, either. Why, it's just honest stealin', that's what bein' a politician is."

"Anyway, he goes on here, 'Once I get power in the capital, Jake, you can count on running Grub Stake as a wide-open city. Gambling, whoring, all the best of everything.' "

"Boy, how the money will roll in then!" Bobby O'Toole enthused.

"You've got the right of that, O'Toole," Tulley told his henchman. "Anything else?"

"Only he asks you to be sure and hurry. No delays can be tolerated, he says."

"You heard the man, fellers. I want you each to ride out today. Round up all the hardcases, road agents, drifters and gunhawks you can and have them meet here three days from now. Boy-oh-boy, I'm gonna have the toughest gang ever seen on the plains when we ride into this Grub Stake. Uh . . . did Roger say where that was?"

"Sure did. It's in the mountains, thirty-five miles north and east of Silver Creek. He also says there's a big fight going on between those what want to keep the capital named Silver Creek and those who believe it should be Denver. Thinks there ought be some profit for us in that difficulty, too."

"So that settles it, boys. Here's to Grub Stake." He hoisted his glass high. "An' here's to the Bitter Creek Jake Tulley gang. We've got us a whole town of our own!"

TWO

Dried blood crusted red-brown on the buckboard. Huge black crows pecked at the eyeballs of the murdered Indian family. Two persons sat their horses in bitter silence, eyeing the grisly scene. One, an attractive, golden-skinned young woman in a supple deer-hide Sioux squaw dress, drew a Smith & Wesson .38 "Baby Russian," revolver from the soft pouch holster at her side. The hammer ratcheted back and she squeezed the trigger.

One of the crows fell dead, in a welter of ebon feathers, while the others flew hastily off, squawking their protest to this invasion.

Her companion, a tall, lean white man in the hunting shirt, buckskin breeches and loincloth of a Crow warrior, his blond hair cut into the roach style of a Strong Heart, nodded in approval. Then he gigged his mount closer.

"White men did this," he observed after inspecting the shod hoof prints on the ground around the wagon. "Tulley's gang?"

"The boy's had his breech cloth jerked down. I'd say it was Bobby O'Toole. He's not particular, so long as they are young," Rebecca Caldwell replied.

"He wasn't ravaged," Lone Wolf informed her.

"Then something interrupted O'Toole."

"Tulley or the rest?"

"No," Rebecca speculated while she examined the

14

area around them. "Two men alone did this. From the turned-out pockets I'd say the motive was robbery. The trail leads on to the southwest. We'll have to make camp soon. By tomorrow we should be close again. I . . . Oh, Lone Wolf, I *hunger* to get my hands on those animals."

"Especially Roger Styles?"

Rebecca's eyes clouded and her anger rose in choking waves when she thought of Roger Styles. She burned with a longing to get him in her sights. The suave master criminal had stripped her and violated her body in a dirty, shameful manner. Now she lived with a new emotion beside her desire for revenge. Humiliation did not sit well upon her broad young shoulders, nor go well with the proud carriage of her aristocratic face. She had inherited her noble bearing and sturdy body from her father, the Sioux chief, Iron Calf, to whom, ironically, she and her mother had been traded five years ago by Jake Tulley and her ne'er-do-well uncles, Ezekial and Virgil Caldwell. Well, at least, she relished with satisfaction, Virgil had paid for his part in the vile business. Her perseverance and classic good features she got from the Scots ancestors of her mother, Hannah Caldwell. Born out of wedlock, as the result of a rape, Rebecca felt doubly degraded by Roger Styles' forced attentions. He would, she vowed, pay more, and longer, than all the rest. Abruptly she shook her shoulders to cast off the chill mood that Lone Wolf's words had brought upon her.

"Yes," she hissed. "Roger most of all."

They trotted along in silence, following the sign left by Bobby O'Toole and another outlaw, who led away with them the two unshod ponies of the murdered Indian family. Rebecca's mind still burned with the image of Roger Styles' pallid, naked body writhing

15

atop her. Rape! How she loathed the word. Yet, she surmised, her own introduction to womanhood, while still a captive and not a wife among the Oglala, had in reality hardly been less . . .

. . . Rebecca Caldwell stood belly deep in the chill water of a creek at the edge of Iron Calf's Oglala village. Her sixteen year old body tingled with excitement. Before her stood an Oglala youth, Four Horns, a boy only two years older than she. Like herself, he was entirely naked.

Suddenly Four Horns stepped closer and she felt the warmth of his long, hard penis press against her lower abdomen. She thrilled to the touch. Her body trembled with anticipation.

"Oh!" she squealed. In an instant, her romantic young girl's heart melted in a flood of desire. She reached out with a hand that lacked conscious direction. Her fingers tightly circled his throbbing shaft and she squeezed with all her might.

"Ah!" Four Horns exclaimed, his body aquiver with delight. "That's more like it."

"Oh . . . Four Horns, I . . ." Rebecca closed her eyes. She threw back her head while a delicious tremor of delight coursed through her nubile body. Slowly she began to stroke him, the loose skin sliding easily while the silken tip inscribed circles on her belly and sent ecstatic shivers through her.

"That's it . . . that's just perfect," Four Horns encouraged.

"But . . . the *akacita?* What if we are caught?"

"I am not afraid of the camp police. If they find us, they will only laugh and make rude jokes. More, my sweet dove. Do it faster."

"What if some little boys find us here?" Rebecca

protested, fear reasserting itself over her desire.

Four Horns only laughed. "Why, they will watch us from hiding and stroke themselves like you are doing for me."

"Four Horns, I . . ." she stammered.

By then it was too late.

Rebecca opened her eyes and watched, fascinated, while Four Horns dipped one hand under the water. She felt his thick fingers grope near her wildly aroused maidenhead. Like sinuous snakes, they brushed against her silken mound, spreading the lips wide before plunging into her sweet core. Her sensitive, moistly eager passage pulsated in welcome.

She sucked in her breath. Never had anything felt so good!

Quaking with a sensation beyond anything her childish experiments had previously engendered, she let Four Horns' questing digits fully enter her, while pulses of pure joy surged out to electrify her fingers and toes.

"Oh . . . my . . . God!" she cried in English, utterly transported. Instantly her hungry, fiery body betrayed her utterly. Her hand flew with greater and greater speed, while she directed the springy shaft she held downward toward that burning cavern where Four Horns worked so industriously. He plunged in and out of it, while his thumb sought and found that small, rigid button she had often teased as a little girl.

His caress quickly stimulated it to a nearly painfully gratifying itch that exceeded anything her own efforts had achieved. She began to writhe in delirious enchantment.

"I . . . don't . . . think . . . we . . . should . . . be . . . doing . . . this . . ." Rebecca panted, her voice nearing a sob. She brought his throbbing phallus into the sparse, wispy strands of her pubic hair, then lower

17

into the top folds of her burning cleft. Deep within, she felt something struggling to explode with a richness that went beyond her wildest romantic fantasies.

Then, abruptly, it ended with the approach of others. The young lovers clung together for another long, passionate moment, bodies nearly joined in the first act of love, then parted.

Later that night, Four Horns had come to the small lodge Rebecca shared with her mother. He slipped in under the lower skirt, where she had loosened it for him. By the dying light of glowing coals she saw the bulge in his loincloth and eagerly undid the flap, releasing his surging love dagger.

When he plunged his raging maleness into her agitated purse of delights she thought she would gladly die the next minute, for surely she had been fulfilled by this glorious pleasure they shared. The pain of her defloration lasted less than the time to describe it and Rebecca entered wholly into the most perfect and delightful experience of her young life with eager abandon.

Twice they coupled that night and the moment Four Horns removed his still-rigid penis from its nesting place, she immediately regretted that it could not remain there forever and mourned its loss. Before the snows fell that winter, she and Four Horns had been married. Rebecca never regretted acting so wantonly when she should have recoiled in modesty . . .

. . . Early the next morning, Rebecca and Lone Wolf located an abandoned stage. Bodies littered the ground.

"Four men . . . not the same we have been

18

following," Lone Wolf remarked as he studied the ground. "But headed the same way."

"Tulley must be calling together more men to increase the size of his gang," Rebecca speculated aloud. "Isn't it strange that bad white men, even when they are on their way to do evil, can't resist the urge to do more? What Sioux, or Cheyenne or Crow warrior, riding to meet others in secret for a war raid would attack someone on the way?"

"Few. Only those who were filled with terrible hate."

Rebecca smiled sadly. "Who are our people, then, Lone Wolf?" She shook off the feeling. "All the tracks lead toward the southeast corner of the state. We had better make a wide sweep and find out how many men are joining Tulley."

"A good idea. If his force is too great, we would have no chance at all."

"There's *always* a chance. We beat them before and we can do it again." Rebecca's mouth formed a grim line.

Two hours later they crossed another trail that led to Chappel, Nebraska. A short distance down the road, a tall plume of smoke rose into the clear prairie air. Rebecca and Lone Wolf rode toward it without speaking. They found the charred remains of a wagon, its contents strewn on the ground, and three bodies.

"Tulley seems to be collecting the worst of a bad lot," Rebecca observed in a hard, flat tone. "Whoever they are, they can't be matched for viciousness."

Oh, yes they could, she thought as they loped across the vast sea of waving buffalo grass. There had been one time, not long after she and her mother had been bartered to the Sioux, when the entire village went to war. The Arikaree had caught and butchered some women and small children of the Hunkpapa Sioux. The call had gone out to all the Sioux Nation for a vengeance raid. It was decided that everyone would, in some way, participate. An involuntary shudder passed through Rebecca when she recalled the result.

"Hear me! Hear me!" the Eyanpaha cried through the village of Iron Calf. "This person has come into our camp to raise the war lance," the camp crier continued.

A handsome, slender young warrior sat astride a gray-speckled war pony, a long lance of many feathers in his left hand, fur-tufted, circular bull hide shield on his arm. He looked stern and exceedingly brave. For all his splendor, his presence struck fear in Rebecca Caldwell.

Oh, God, more burned farms, scalped men and women and perhaps more captives. Beside her, Hannah Caldwell trembled. Would it never end, never be the same?

"Many hands of women and children of our brothers, the Hunkpapa, have been murdered by our ancient enemy, the *Palani*. This person calls for all-out war on this enemy. This person is a *Cante Tinza*. He asks those who would take up the lance with him to step forward. If one man goes, the entire camp of Iron Calf will go on the warpath. The *blotahunka* have been consulted and all agree in this. Who will go? Who will go?"

Great excitement coursed through the village as six young warriors raced each other to be first to touch the visitor's lance and pledge their support. The craze infected everyone. Women rushed forward, hacked off one braid and swore to fight like a man. Small boys seized their rabbit bows and shot blunt arrows into the air, yelling in shrill voices to each other about the deeds of bravery they would perform.

The young man from the Brave Heart warrior society took it in with a passive expression, his eyes amused. A shiver of terror sped through Rebecca at this display of savagery. She knew even then that this image would be forever impressed on her mind. Two days later the order was given to strike camp.

Within a week, bands of *Minikayawozupi*—the Miniconjou—of *Ihanktonwan*—the Yankton—and *Titonwan*—the Titon—traveled along with their Oglala brothers in a mighty caravan that went deep into Arikara country. Late one afternoon, the scouts rode to announce that a *Palani* village had been sighted. Preparations for battle began at once.

"We attack at the coming of tomorrow's sun," Walks Little, the raid chief, announced in each circle of lodges. "But first we steal the *Palani* horses. For this I need two hands of boys from each camp. Those chosen will come to me at the setting of the sun."

Rebecca watched, inwardly horrified, while Walks Little selected ten boys from Iron Calf's village, all of them between ten and fourteen years of age. Those picked armed themselves from the weapons of their fathers or older brothers and, puffed with pride, strode about the milling throng of people until called to eat a hasty evening meal.

Everyone was to have a role in the upcoming conflict, Rebecca discovered. The boys would steal the Arikara horses in the last hour of darkness. The warriors of the enemy would swarm after them, leaving only a few to guard the village. Then the bulk of the Sioux warriors would strike at the poorly defended camp. Others, chosen for their bravery, would hold the hostile fighting men while the encampment was burned and the occupants killed.

21

Before the conflict ended, the women and children would also enter the fray to finish the slaughter. Rebecca quailed at the thought. At fifteen, the idea of taking a human life appalled her. Not so, the Oglala girls of her age.

"Oh, it will be a great fight," Bird Song enthused. "I can hardly wait until my knife drinks *Palani* blood."

"Will . . . will I have to kill them, too?" Rebecca asked, afraid that she knew the answer.

"No. But you'll want to cut off a few noses, some ears, lips," Bird Song replied. She smacked her lips as though savoring a tasty buffalo stew.

"Think of it, *Śinaskawin*," Red Shawl added. "This raid will be remembered and sung about through all times to come. And the evil *Palani* will never again kill our women and children."

"But they weren't . . . ah, *our* women and children," Rebecca protested. "They were Hunkpapa."

"All the same, they were *Lakotah*, that is what counts."

When day was a thin gray line on the horizon, the attack began. Each contingent had been moved into position, even the smallest children remaining silent. The small Sioux boys slipped into the horse herd. Since this was a vengeance raid, the Arikara boys guarding the ponies died silently, their throats slit in the traditional Sioux manner. Then the lithe youngsters leaped astride chosen mounts and uttered wild whoops of joy. The startled *Palani* animals stampeded.

Instantly, an alarm sounded in the sleeping village. Men ran out, many naked, clutching whatever sort of weapon they had closest at hand. They ran swiftly after their disappearing horses. And directly into a

22

flurry of arrows loosed by Sioux warriors. More Arikara fighting men joined the surprise battle, until only a dozen or so remained behind with the women, children and old people. At that moment, Walks Little howled out his war cry and the bulk of the Sioux raiders fell on the confused encampment.

Death screams soon overrode shouted questions and the smell of blood and voided bowels rose in the dusty air. Flames began to leap from buffalo hide lodges and the occupants shrieked in terror. Many, who feared to expose themselves to the war clubs, lances and arrows of the vengeful Sioux, remained inside to be burned to death. Others fell to swift blows and feathered shafts, while children ran aimlessly around the camp. Then the signal came for the women and children to join in.

Shrill voices rose in imitation of the warriors' war cries and the Sioux women fell upon the stunned survivors of the Arikara village. Sickened by the brutal scene, Rebecca gagged and turned away, only to see a long, metal trade knife plunging toward her bosom.

Instinctively, she blocked it with her left forearm and thrust outward with the skinning knife in her right hand. The tip pierced the skin on the eleven-year-old knife-wielder's chest. A rib deflected it and Rebecca watched with revulsion as the blade sliced a long, curving gash in his flesh before it came free. Then she bent double and vomited when bits of his brain matter, bone chips and blood splashed her face and arms. A tall Sioux warrior had smashed the child's skull with a heavy war club. Around her the fight raged on.

"The Sioux beadwork on your dress saved your life, *waśiwin*," the warrior told her roughly a moment later. "That and the way you cut up that *Palani* dog." He smiled briefly and disappeared into the fray.

Numbed, Rebecca sought escape from the horror in the outer darkness.

A blood-red sun rose, bloated, on the horizon and hung two hands span high before the killing ended. The most terrible part, to Rebecca's thinking, had been the pitiful screams of the dying children.

"They are just children," Lone Wolf said in disgust. "I am ashamed to have been born white when I see this sort of thing."

"I know what you mean," Rebecca replied, shaken out of her reverie by the sudden appearance of a burned house, its occupants brutally murdered and left lying in the blazing sunlight. "There is no doubt that white men did this and I'm sure they are headed for wherever Tulley is hiding."

"I've seen enough of this."

"So have I. Let's go after Tulley. I only hope that we can catch up to him and settle our score before any more innocents suffer at the hands of that gang."

THREE

Soft, sweet-scented breeze soughed through the long needles of tall, thick-trunked pines. Woodpeckers alternately rapped on the scaly bark for grubs to eat and shrilly scolded the long column of men who rode along the rutted track below. Their anger over this invasion of the peaceful Colorado mountains by twenty-six scruffy, hard-bitten men would have been increased a hundred fold if they knew the purpose that directed the interlopers.

"Grub Stake's up ahead about three miles," Luke Wellington told Bitter Creek Jake.

"Good. We'll be there before suppertime," the bandit leader commented. "That way, by the time the boiled spuds's passed a second time, we'll own the town."

"Don't be too sure of that, Jake," Wellington offered. "These miners are kinda tough. Some of 'em fought in the War and they're not afraid to pull the trigger on a man."

"Huh!" Rupe Denton exploded. "You turnin' yeller in your old age, Wellington? Why, this is gonna be like taking candy from a toddler." One long, artist's finger smoothed the thin line of black mustache that adorned Denton's upper lip. His nearly colorless gray eyes held a mocking challenge.

"Ain't seen the day I couldn't take you, Rupe," Luke returned. "Just that I know miners. 'Least the sort we saw sneakin' into the Black Hills, against the treaty law."

With a shake of his scraggly blond hair, Clyde Morton gigged his mount forward and joined the conversation. "You line me up five of those miners, see? And they're going down, *bang! bang! bang!* just like that."

Rupe sneered at the young gunhawk. "Grow up, kid. If any of them get a chance to buck us, it'll be from behind logs and up trees and inside mine tunnels. Luke's right about them being tough. But the way I figure it, we've got surprise on our side and for sure, Jake's got a plan to make use of that."

"You won the cigar, Denton," Tulley said through a smile. He liked flattery, though he accepted it as his due, not for what it really was. "Six of us will ride in and size up the law-dog situation. If everything seems peaceful enough, we signal the rest and you hightail it in and we start talkin' over."

"What's the signal?" Morton asked.

"Oh, you won't be able to miss it. It'll be gunshots."

Ken Spires stood at the bar in Peterson's Mother Lode saloon and took a deep draught of a foam-capped beer in a huge glass schooner. Ah, how good it felt, he rejoiced, after a day of tasting rock dust and stale water. He carefully eyed the strangers when they entered through the batwings, lids slitted in a miner's natural distrust. They looked like hardcases to him. Especially the big one with the beer belly and pistol butt stuck in his belt close to his hand for a fast cross-draw.

"Howdy," the big, square-jawed man addressed Rolf Peterson, who stood behind the bar. "Can you tell me where I can find your badge?"

"We don't have a lawman in Grub Stake," Peterson returned.

"That so? Don't sound like too safe a proposition to me. What do you do when there's trouble?"

"Not much of that here. There is a miner's council, of course. If someone does something bad, a hearing can always be arranged. That usually gets the offender run out of town. If what he did was really awful, there's a squat pine at the edge of town with a low, sturdy limb. We can always scare up rope enough and men to use it."

Spires watched while an incredibly fat man next to the talkative stranger reach unconsciously to a wide swath of bandanna that circled his neck. That one's come close to hangin' before, Spires concluded. For that matter, they all looked like gallows meat.

"Ya don't say?" the apparent leader went on. A lanky, stringbean of a man, with long, reddish-blond locks, detached himself from the group and ambled toward the bar. He stopped a few feet from Ken Spires.

"Ain't you a little young to be drinkin' with growed-up men, Sonny?" Luke Wellington addressed Ken Spires.

Spires flushed crimson. His youthful appearance had always seemed an advantage, certainly not a matter for ridicule. "I'm old enough," he muttered. "If it's any business of yours."

Dangerous fires flickered in Wellington's eyes. "What was that you said?"

"Nothing," Spires replied softly, suddenly reluctant to push this issue. Beyond his tormentor, the other hardcase spoke again.

"Well, now, no marshal, is it? Seems this place is ripe for a little law and order. The name's Tulley. Bitter Creek Jake Tulley. Perhaps you've heard of me."

27

Although only a dozen-odd early drinkers, from the early shift or owners of their own claims, occupied the Mother Lode, three of them looked up, faces wearing expressions of shock. Two of them gasped aloud.

"Ah, I see my fame has arrived ahead of me," Tulley gloated. "Well, you boys seem in need of a law-dog and I've sorta decided it's gonna be me. A man needs to change his ways, so to speak, from time to time. To be of service to his fellow humans. So, from now on, I run Grub Stake for our mutual benefit." A hoarse bellow of laughter followed.

"An' first off is to take care of somethin' that's an offense to public decency," Luke Wellington spoke up. "I don't like that pretty-boy face you got, feller," he said to Spires. "Your eyes is too close together and you got a lopsided mouth. Them freckles is the worst part. Looks like you've been standin' behind a cow eatin' bran. You're gonna have to leave this town, Sonny."

"I'll not be doin' that," Spires protested. "I have a job, a home, a wife . . ." his mouth snapped shut when Wellington put up a warning hand.

"You got a gun on, Sonny?"

"N-no," Spires stammered.

"Then you'd best be gettin' one. Hey, Jake, lend this li'l boy that spare iron of yours."

"Glad to, Deputy Wellington."

"*Luke Wellington?*" The name sent icy prongs down Spires' spine. He had heard the name often. A cold, conscienceless killer.

Tulley pulled the old Remington from his waistband and handed it to Luke, who laid it on the bar and gave the revolver a slight shove, so that it ended up near Ken's hand with a musical clink when the barrel struck his beer glass.

"Where do you want it, Sonny? In here or out in the street."

"I . . . I . . . why, I'm not gonna go against you, Mr. Wellington."

"Oh, yes you are. Right here and now, if you don't walk out into the street."

"B-but I ain't done nothin' to you."

"Yes, you have. Your face offends me. Didn't you hear?"

Spires stifled a groan of abject misery, watching his life gallop away from him like a spooked team. He thought of his wife, Ellen, of the baby on the way and the money he had worked so hard to save so that they could live in peace and comfort. It couldn't end. Not now. The war had taken his father from the family and, to escape grinding poverty, he had left home at the age of seventeen to make a place for himself and be able to send cash home to help his mother and younger sisters. He couldn't let some loudmouthed gunslick stop all that now when he had a real chance to do all he'd dreamed of.

His hands flicked out and the work-callused fingers closed around the polished walnut grips of the Remington.

Two shots roared from Luke's Colt before Spires got his thumb wrapped over the hammer. The first slammed him back against the bar when it smashed into his chest. The second snapped his head back when it burst his heart. Ken Spires was dead before his body hit the rough plank floor. A cloud of sawdust rose around his twitching form.

"Well, boys," Tulley spoke into the silence that followed, "let's go tell the other businessmen that law and order has come to Grub Stake."

"What's that shootin' about?" a bearded miner shouted ahead of him as he ran down the street, a long barreled shotgun in his hands.

Bitter Creek Jake and his owlhoots stood in the

29

muddy street. From behind them, at the door of the Mother Lode, a voice called out in explanation.

"That there feller just gunned down poor Ken Spires. His name's Luke Wellington."

"I don't care if it be Satan hisself! Damn you, Mister, Ken was a friend of mine." The long tubes of the Greener started to swing toward Luke.

Three outlaw guns spoke as one. The bullets ripped and tore into the miner. He staggered backward, blood pumping from a wound in one thigh, two in his chest. He dropped the shotgun and his eyes rolled up in his head. "Marthie! Marthie!" he cried out to his long-dead wife. "I'm hurt bad."

Then he crashed to the mire of the main street of Grub Stake and his legs twitched out the last of his life.

With wild hoots and hollers, the rest of the Tulley gang rode into town. Tulley quickly organized them and sent each pair to visit the local business establishments. He and Luke Wellington turned back to the Mother Lode and the bandit chief addressed his next remarks to the owner.

"You been right hospitable to me, Mister, ah . . ."

"Peterson."

"On that account, I'm gonna make you a right generous offer, Mr. Peterson. This here establishment of yours looks like it would make a right nice jail and city hall. An' a headquarters for my boys. I'll buy it from you and pay you a fair price."

"I'm sorry, it's not for sale."

"How's that? I don't think you heard me. I said I was gonna *buy* the Mother Lode and make it into a real civic attraction. When I offer to buy something, it's never refused."

"It is this time, *Mister* Tulley. The Mother Lode is not for sale."

"Luke . . . convince the man."

Wellington's Colt slid into his hand. The first bullet struck Rolf Peterson in the left kneecap. He rebounded off the clapboard front of his saloon and clutched a low rail for support. Luke took casual aim and shot Peterson in the right shoulder.

"Hope you're left-handed, Mr. Peterson," Tulley smirked. "You're gonna have to sign the title."

"N-never," Rolf Peterson managed to gasp out.

Tulley gave Luke a significant nod.

Luke's third slug struck Peterson a fraction of an inch above the bridge of his nose. His eyes bulged and a wet spray of blood, fluids and brain matter erupted from the back of his skull to splatter the unpainted wall of the Mother Lode.

"Yep. Reckon I just saved me the cash price of this place. Let's start movin' in, boys."

Recently oiled hinges gave no betraying squeak when the door opened briefly to let a dark figure slip inside. The dim light showed only a second before the nail-studded plank shut out the night.

"Glad you could make it, Bart," a grizzled hard rock miner said softly. He ran thick, stubby fingers through his curly black beard. "Ev'rbody's here now."

"Sometimes, I can't believe all this is happening," Bart Carstairs offered in a husky voice. He ducked his five foot eleven frame under a low beam and found a chair. Quickly he took in the other people in the room.

Kathlene O'Day, stout, buxom, determined. Owning the Silver Creek Cafe, he knew she would be here. Of course, Matt Peterson. After the murder of his father, he and Hard Rock Mike had called this meeting. And Tom Allison. The big blacksmith would be sure to side with them against the Tulley gang. Together they comprised the solid citizenry of Grub Stake. It had been Tom Allison and the late Rolf Peterson who had come to him and proposed he run for mayor when the town had its first elections two months in the future. He had been flattered and pleased to accept. At forty-five he had done a bit of everything.

As a youth he had ridden the Pony Express, until the telegraph had put them out of business. He fought for the Union in the War Between the States, as an infantry officer. He'd seen a lot of action there, killed more men than he liked to think about. Afterward, he had sort of drifted. Tried his hand as a highwayman for a while. He reflected on the experience in sour regret. The men he had been forced to associate with had not been to his liking and the things they had to do to make a living on the owlhoot trail had gone against the grain. Then, wounded, abandoned by his fellow outlaws, he had experienced a sort of revelation. Bart "got religion." When, as it seemed to him, he was miraculously found and cared for by a kind, Christian family, he swore off his old ways, moved to Colorado Territory and took up work as a clerk in a Silver Creek haberdashery. Before long he handled the books, made all orders from traveling drummers and the eastern catalogs. He met and married Laura Wade, became a partner in the business, prospered and then moved on to Grub Stake when the new strike came.

The new boomtown seemed an answer to his prayers. At least until that afternoon, when Bitter Creek Jake Tulley and his gang stormed into town and took over. Bart brought his rambling thoughts back under control when he realized that Hard Rock Mike Hoxsey had started talking.

"It's certain," the miner said through his beard, "that all of us are agreed that we can't let this Tulley come in and take over our town. Why, the way I hear it now, every merchant, mine owner, tradesman is supposed to pay for the 'support' of our new police department . . . which means Tulley and his gunslingers. Next thing you know, he'll come after the small claims and anybody else that can be scared into paying up."

"Don't forget that they are killers. Look at what happened to my father." Young Matt Peterson switched his cobalt gaze from one person to the next. "All Dad said was that he wouldn't sell and . . . they shot him down for it. I want to see them pay for that. I want Wellington hanged and the rest jailed or dead. I'm not a gunhand, but I can shoot well enough to help."

"In that case, why don't you wait in a dark alley tomorrow night and backshoot Wellington?" Mike Hoxsey suggested.

"No. I want him swinging from a rope." The vehemence behind his words made his dark blue eyes glow. Matt ran a small hand through his nearly white blond hair and licked his lips.

"If I can get my two cents worth in here, I've got somethin' to add."

"Go right ahead, Katie," Hard Rock Mike invited.

"Sure an' this reminds me o' the black-hearted English lords and toffs it does. It's all but bandits they are, too. The only way to not lose out to that kind is to leave, like so many of us did from Ireland, or to fight, which many o' the brave lads is doin' right now. Me, I've done all the runnin' I've a mind to. I say we organize and fight."

"Hear, hear!" Tom Allison added forcefully. "Tulley is an outlaw. His men are the worst looking lot

33

I've ever encountered. They're killers all, on that we agree. We have to fight, but can we hope to succeed?"

"I don't know," Matt Peterson admitted, a reluctant shrug making him look younger than his twenty-two years. "But I'm willing to give it a try. Tulley isn't the law. Not real law like a town should have. My only wish is that there was someone, somewhere who could come and help us."

"Ezekial, I'm putting you in charge of the entertainment in this place," Jake Tulley told the corrupt Caldwell. He waved an arm to take in the Mother Lode saloon. "We want good likker, pretty women and honest gamblers. By that last, I mean those who make a good split of their take with the house. With that shot-up arm of yours, you'd not do so well on the rough house side of our little deal."

"That's generous of you, of course, Jake," Ezekial replied. "Though you know I'm willing as the next to deal with the miners and the like."

"No. You have a special talent for things like this saloon. Who do you know who can keep the girls in line?"

A distant look lighted Ezekial's eyes a moment, then his lips curled in a cruel, though satisfied smile. "I have just the one. She has . . . a special talent for that. Flora Belle Chase. She gives her girls little balls of opium to keep them in line and willing to work. If that don't do it, she also is a top hand with a whip. She lays it on with a will and in such a manner that it doesn't interfere with them working on their backs. Two days with Flora Belle and she could get a nun to fuck."

Clyde Morton, who leaned against one wall of Tulley's appropriated office, snickered and the gang

34

leader, himself, let out a snort of amusement. "Sounds like what we need. Send for her, if you would. How long before you think she can be here?"

"I'm not sure of that. Last I heard, she was runnin' a string of girls down Santa Fe way. I'll have to go somewhere to send a wire. Whatever the case, we can start recruiting right away."

"With you, of course, sampling all the merchandise to make certain of its quality, eh, Zeke?"

"Can you name anyone better, Jake?"

"How about Bobby O'Toole?" Morton offered.

"Shut up, Clyde," Jake snapped. "You ask me, you're getting to be as sick as O'Toole. Now, Ezekial, we ought to lay some plans for the event that that niece of yours tracks us here."

"What for? We got the whole town in our hands. One sight of that little bitch and she gets her brains splattered on Main Street."

FOUR

Ezekial Caldwell, Jake Tulley, Bobby O'Toole, Luke Wellington: The names and the evil faces that went with them were deeply burned into the surface of Rebecca Caldwell's mind. While she made her solitary camp and laid wood for a cook fire, she reflected again on that awful day, now nearly six years in the past, when she and her mother had become pawns in a deadly game of trade between Iron Calf's Oglala and the Tulley gang.

Her uncles, Ezekial and Virgil, had become ne'er-do-wells and readily drifted into the fringes of a criminal lifestyle. Their association with Jake Tulley had been irregular up until then. Once the dreadful bargain had been struck, with whiskey, arms and the two women in exchange for the lives of the outlaws, the brothers had thrown in entirely with Tulley and his schemes. What followed for Rebecca had been five years of abject misery and horror.

No, that was not so, she chided herself while she contemplated a quick wash-up in the shallow creek that flowed near her camp. Her thoughts filled with the image of Four Horns, lean, muscular frame and handsome features, her husband and lover. There had been good times, too. Quickly she removed her clothing and stepped into the chill, snow-melt waters of the Rocky Mountain stream.

At nineteen, Rebecca Caldwell had matured into a

fully developed woman. By the standards of her time, she could not be called voluptuous, yet she had full, pertly up-thrust breasts, a delightful curving inlet to her narrow waist and the proud flare of hips that insured an excellent child bearer. Her legs were sturdy and muscular from years of walking long distances and from riding horses astride, Indian style, rather than in a properly modest sidesaddle. They remained well-turned and shapely, though. Rebecca had been born to her mother, Hannah, after a violent sexual assault that had been part of a minor raid by the Sioux. During her captivity, Rebecca learned that this particular warrior had become the powerful Oglala chief, Iron Calf, who had taken mother and daughter under his protection . . . if it could be called that. This infusion of Sioux blood had given her long, silky raven hair, high cheekbones and a light golden complexion that darkened only slightly, and most attractively, with exposure to the sun.

From her Caldwell ancestors, she had inherited deep, sparkling blue eyes and a flawless skin texture. Also the Scots tenacity to withstand any hardship and benefit from it. She and Four Horns had made love for the first time only a few days after her sixteenth birthday. Four months later, they were married. Both the boy, only two years her senior, and Chief Iron Calf gave away many horses in honor of the celebration and the young couple settled down to a promised happy future. Rebecca crouched down in the water and thought of the year and a half they had while the gurgling stream brushed sensuously against her flesh, arousing the fires of her passion. Ah, Four Horns, Four Horns, she summoned from memory. How magnificent the way you could transport me to the peaks of ecstasy . . .

* * *

. . . There had been a big buffalo surround. The hunters had downed many hands of the shaggy beasts and the women labored from before sunup to long after sunset for five long days to tend the meat. The hides had been scraped and set aside for their later attention. Rebecca, along with the other wives, had prepared special, succulent portions of the animals for their menfolk. Her body ached with fatigue and her fingers had grown stiff and swollen. Yet her heart quickened when Four Horns came to her and spoke a suggestion in the soft tones of love.

"You are covered with blood, my little dove. And so am I, and the dust of hunting. Come, let us go to the creek. I will help you wash clean of your labor and you can do the same for me."

"And then . . . ?" Rebecca teased in the Sioux language.

"We shall see." Four Horns grinned whitely and reached to help her to her feet. "Yes, I think for certain we shall see."

They located an isolated spot, screened and protected by drooping red willows and clattering young cottonwoods. Rebecca quickly shed her blood-stiffened doeskin dress and posed, ankle deep and invitingly naked, in the warm summer waters of the creek.

"Oh, this is wonderful. Exactly what I need," she enthused.

Four Horns dropped his hunting leggings of thick bull hide and removed his buckskin loin cloth. The moment the soft, tepid breeze caressed his long penis, it rapidly swelled to rigid fullness. He stepped close to Rebecca, until his burning shaft touched the slight swell of her newly pregnant abdomen. Its contact sent shivers of delight through the young girl.

"I have something else you need right here," he

murmured in her ear. His tongue darted out and traced the curling pattern beyond the lobe.

"Aaah, Four Horns. No matter how hard we worked, I always thought about this moment." She reached down and gently encircled his bulging maleness. Slowly she began to stroke it.

"This is like . . . like the first time we expressed our love for each other," Rebecca gasped out.

"Yes. Only you were not smelly with days of butchering and caked with blood." He gave her a gentle push so that she fell over backward into the creek.

"Four Horns! You're awful!" she cried in English. Then she began to laugh. He joined her while he returned to the shore to fetch a lump of the fat root with yellow skin — a mixture of yucca and soapweed used to care for hair and skin. Then he launched himself full length into the water and paddled to Rebecca's side.

Tenderly he washed her clean, both of them thrilling to how the gentle strokes and cleansing action of water and root mixture heightened their desire. When Four Horns finished his wife's bath, he lazed back in the water and indicated that she should do the same for him.

"What if I don't want to?" Rebecca pouted. "And what do I do with this *sluka?*" She pointed to his erect penis that extended several inches above the water.

"Give it good care, little dove, very special care."

With practiced skill, she used both hands and the natural soap to clean his lean, muscular body. She gave special attention to the scars that denoted his participation in the sundance and then bent to kiss his nipples, which hardened with a speed to match her own. Her firm, girl's breasts brushed his chest and he sighed while she worked lower. When the ablution ended, she returned her attention to his turgid manhood, that still thrust above the water.

At first she encased it in both hands and stroked rapidly until the delightful tingling sensation caused Four Horns to arch his back and rise out of the water, poised on his broad shoulders and heels. Then she bent forward, her braids dragging across his taut belly and bringing him more delight, and surrounded the fat, purplish tip with her full, sweet lips.

She held the kiss until he cried out in ecstasy, the tip of her tongue tracing small circles over the sensitive flesh.

"Aaaah! You've learned. You've learned so well," he crooned. "It tickles so much it hurts."

In a furious swirl of water, like a giant catfish, Rebecca changed her position, legs astride his narrow waist, and lowered her own hot, moist flesh toward the thick bulk of his maleness. With painstaking languor, she slid his throbbing shaft past the frilly pink folds and guided it deep inside the slithery passage to her soul-burning core.

"Th-the baby," he started in half-hearted protest. Rebecca silenced him with a finger across his lips.

"It is all right, my love. The other girls tell me it will be safe for at least two moons more. Oh, how I want you. All of you. Deep inside me and filling me. Now! Now! Oh, yes, even more!"

Four Horns began to undulate his hips, thrusting with all his strength against the rhythmic contractions of the muscles that controlled her silken purse. There is no other, no other girl like her, he thought, his heart pounding, not one in the whole of the earth.

"Wonderful!" Rebecca cried out in English. And, yes it was a wonder. Like a miracle, this tingling, sense-jarring blending of two persons into one. Oh, how grand! Why, oh why had she waited so long? Her body, wise as Mother Eve, had been hinting at the marvels to come, making her ache for fulfillment for over five years. If it was always so good, why had she waited? Would . . . would it always be so good? For an instant her heart skipped a beat, unsure of her future.

Then bright rockets burst, like over Fort Henry, and she gave herself fully to the indescribable pleasure they shared. Four Horns drove himself faster and faster, then paused a long ten heart beats, fully driven into her warm cave of pungent nectar, then began again, slowly, building until both of them keened out their mutual delight.

A savageness seemed to possess them both. Four Horns bit at her shoulder and she clawed his back, though her broken and bitten off nails left no tell-tale scars. She could feel the long, thick pole of flesh grinding into her innermost secret place and the joy rising in her breast until she could contain it no longer. With an abandoned whinny she peaked and her life force gushed.

Dictated by nature, more than experience, Four Horns carefully paced himself, holding off his own rushing completion, until Rebecca bit her lower lip and threw back her head. Her heavy black braids thrashed from side to side as she heaved about in transported delirium as she surged up the slope to another crashing climax.

With a final surge of rapid strokes Four Horns brought them together to the precipice, and over into mutual nirvana.

Oh . . . oh . . . oh . . . how . . . good . . . it felt! Rebecca exulted in triumph . . .

. . . Rebecca Caldwell, former captive of the Sioux

41

and questor after vengeance returned abruptly to the present to find her hand frantically manipulating the sensitive button at the gate to her secret treasure. Sticky with her juices, her facile fingers quickly brought her to a thunderous, if incomplete, release. She sighed forlornly, replete in the physical sense, but missing Four Horns, or any man who could satisfy her. Why not Lone Wolf? The sensuous corridors of her mind echoed mockingly.

Her companion's vow to seek the Power road required abstinence, she knew, and prohibited any intimacy between them. Yet, she was young and healthy and a woman and her needs cried out. A distant, furtive noise shattered her mood and instantly placed her on the alert. What was it?

There. Her horse, the beautiful sorrel gelding, Ike, nickered in irritation and warning. Someone had to be near the camp. Rebecca's head slid below the surface and she used an underwater breast stroke to close on the bank. Quietly she eased out of the creek and donned her beaded elkskin dress. She bent low and slid her well-shaped feet into moccasins. Lastly she took up her bead-and-quill decorated purse and stole quietly through the low undergrowth back toward her encampment.

"Lookie here, Norm," a voice came to her in a rough stage whisper. "Girlie things. Maybe bein' late to jine up with Bitter Creek Jake weren't so bad a thing after all."

"Yeah. No sign of a man around. You don't think . . . naw, no white gal would be runnin' around without some escort."

"That may be, but this sure's hell's bloomers and a undershift. Nice ridin' habit, too. Purty colors. We's got us some poon for sure, you ask me."

Rebecca crouched behind a screening mountain

laurel and sized up the two scruffy roadagents who had stumbled upon her camp. Norm was rail-thin, his cheeks hollow, complexion wan and slightly yellowish. His companion had a layer of lard around his middle, thickening into a beer belly at the front. He had bandy legs and cold, cruel eyes that flicked constantly around the paraphernalia laid out for the night.

"Wonder where she went, Hiram," Norm expounded.

"Maybe to pee. Or she might be at the crick takin' a bath." Lasciviousness dripped from each word.

"Hey! Iffin she's skinny dippin', that's for me. Be the first time I dipped my wick in the water."

"Wherever we catch her, we's gonna do some humpin'!" Norm declared in return.

Rebecca stepped into the clearing, hips swaying invitingly, right hand dipped into her beaded purse. Neither man saw her at first.

"There's an empty hols . . ." Hiram began, lifting his discovery. He broke off at sight of Rebecca.

"Hot damn! Now we're gonna have some sweet fucking!" he bellowed in delight.

"You'll have to clear that with me, first, boys," Rebecca told them sweetly.

Then she pulled her .38 caliber, double-action Smith & Wesson from the purse. The Baby Russian roared twice, the shots so close as to sound like one.

Both slugs entered Norm's open, gaping mouth. They ripped his tongue from its fauces and a great stream of blood gushed down his esophagus and filled his lungs. Drowned in his own gore, he fell to the ground. Rebecca tracked the muzzle of her revolver toward Hiram.

"Hey! Hey, now, lady! We didn't mean no harm. We was only funnin'." Hiram extended both arms, hands empty and palms turned toward her in supplication. Then the clothes she wore registered on his frightened, coward's brain. "You're an Injun, huh? Well, then, what's all the fuss about? You're used to havin' a bunch o' bucks forked between yer legs, right? What say you an' me make a little push-push?"

Hiram formed a circle of one thumb and index finger and thrust another digit into it, his lips curled in a lewd sneer.

"I wouldn't touch your stinking body with a slop jar."

"Uppity, huh? Well, we'll see about that."

Hiram started forward, then stopped abruptly. A tremendous pain jolted through his groin, as though someone had kicked him in the nuts. In the same instant he heard the report of Rebecca's Baby Russian and discovered the terrifying truth. His body sagged and he dropped to his knees, both hands clutching the agony in his crotch, while blood flowed between his fingers.

"Oh! Oh-oh-oh, God, why'd you do it?" he blubbered, large tears running down his face. Hiram groaned and rocked back and forth. "You ruint me! Why, oh, why?"

"You won't need it where you're going," Rebecca told Hiram a second before she shot him between the eyes.

Two less for Tulley, she thought, reloading her Smith with care. Lone Wolf would approve, she thought with satisfaction.

Suddenly she missed the tall white warrior, wanted him there to smile and comfort her. Nonsense, her mind snapped at her. You don't need coddling. Yet, she did wonder how he had done scouting out the boomtown of Grub Stake.

* * *

"I ain't doin' no such thing, you sumbitch!" a bowlegged, bent-back miner growled at the trio standing in front of him. A fist lashed out with pole-axe force against his jaw. The salt-and-pepper beard snapped to one side and the miner went to his knees.

Lone Wolf watched from deep in the pines, crouched low behind a boulder. He had been following Tulley's men for half a day, making note of their activities. When he reported to Rebecca, he knew her blood would boil and she would want to take action, alone if necessary, to prevent further depredations by the gang she blamed herself for not finishing in the buffalo stampede a month past.

"Dig the wax outtin yer ears, you old fart. I said you was gonna sign this claim over to Mr. Tulley all nice and legal like. Now that's what you're gonna do."

"Go to hell, you ignorant lump of shit!"

A boot toe slammed into the defiant miner's ribs and knocked him onto his back. Tulley's spokesman tried again, his artificial patience exhausted.

"Sign it, or they'll carry you off thisen hill feet first," he threatened.

"Go fuck yourself."

In a blurring instant, the gunhawk filled his hand with a Colt's butt. The big .45 roared and the miner jerked at the impact of the slug. He twitched and groaned, then made a feeble attempt to crawl to safety. The second bullet hit him low in the back and pulverized his left kidney. The dead man plowed dirt with his front teeth, kicked his legs for a second, then went rigid and surrendered to oblivion.

"Awh, shit. Now you gotta sign for him, Lem."

"How's that? I cain't do more'n make my mark."

"Then you, Joe?"

"Sure, Linc."

Suddenly a small boy burst from hiding in a cluster

of rocks and sprinted downhill too fast for the heavier men to react. Silently Lone Wolf followed behind the lad. At the edge of town, the child's sobs of grief and terror found voice in shouted words.

"They killed him! They killed my Paw! That Linc Bascomb gunned him down in cold blood."

"What's this, boy?" Jake Tulley growled when the youngster started to run past the Mother Lode. Jake reached out and arrested the child's flight with a ham fist clamped on his thin shoulder. "What you sayin'?"

"It's true. Linc Bascomb shot my Paw. Murdered him!" again the little boy began to shake with powerful sobs that heaved from deep in his skinny chest.

"Well, then, we'll just have to do something about that, won't we? You know who I am?"

"No, sir."

"I'm Jake Tulley. I'm the law around here now. Looks like we'll have to hold a trial for Mr. Bascomb."

The tow-headed lad's eyes went wide and the freckles on his soft, round cheeks stretched tightly when his jaw dropped. "B-but . . . but Bascomb works for you, don't he?" he inquired in amazement.

"All the same, there'll be a trial, all nice and legal."

Ten minutes later, Linc Bascomb, Lem and Joe returned to Grub Stake. Lone Wolf watched from the concealment of a narrow alleyway. An excited crowd had gathered. Tulley stepped into the center of the street and raised a hand to signal a halt.

"That's far enough, boys. What's this I hear that you've been bushwhackin' miners in cold blood, Linc?"

Bascomb looked down at the ground and scuffed the dust with the toe of one boot. "Awh, now, Jake, that ain't it at all. Ya'see this feller, he . . . he drew on me. I had to defend myself."

"That ain't so," the miner's son challenged in a shrill voice. "He didn' even own a hand iron. Just his Winchester."

"Well . . . well, then, that's what he used," Bascomb took it up. "It was self defense. An' . . . these two fellers was there with me, saw it all. They can tell you."

"All the same, it looks like we have to have a trial," Tulley announced in a cynical tone. "You six, you can be the jury." He indicated members of the gang, including Bobby O'Toole.

He pointed to Ezekial Caldwell, who stood in the doorway to the Mother Lode. "An' you can handle the defense, 'Zekial. Now, then, what about a prosecutor? Ah! I have it." Again Tulley extended an ominous finger.

"Mister Carstairs. You're a learned man, would-be mayor an' all that. You stand for the prosecution."

"This is a travesty, Tulley. I'll not be a part of it," Carstairs growled back.

Tulley shrugged. "Well, then, who? Don't you want to see justice done, Mister Almost Mayor?"

"Please, Mr. Carstairs," the mop-headed boy appealed. "Please." Tears continued to run down his face.

"All right, Timmy. But there'll be no justice, I warn you all. Not so long as this . . . this putrid malefactor keeps you cowered and submissive."

"Watch them words, Mr. Carstairs, or you might be joinin' li'l Timmy's Pap in the graveyard," Luke Wellington snarled.

Carstairs braced himself and ignored Wellington's threat. "What about a judge? The circuit rider for the Territorial Court won't be through for two weeks."

"Why, I sort of figured I'd be the judge," Jake Tulley replied in a wounded tone. "Unless someone thinks me unfit."

"Would it matter?" Carstairs muttered under his breath.

"All right, Mr. Prosecutor. Are you ready to put on your case?"

Carstairs looked startled, his voice incredulous as he gestured around him at the dusty main street of Grub Stake. "Here? You mean right out here on the street?"

"Don't see why not. Trial's supposed to be public, ain't it? Now get on with it."

"Yes, Mr. Tulley. I'd like a moment to confer with my witness."

"Go ahead."

"Come along with me, Timmy."

Five minutes later the clothing merchant and the little boy returned. Carefully, Carstairs put Timmy through the questions, drawing from him all about the threats, the beating of his father, more threats to sign over his claim and lastly the brutal murder. When the lad finished, Carstairs worked his mouth helplessly for a moment, made a futile gesture and concluded.

"That's all for the prosecution."

"Your honor," Luke Wellington growled.

"Your *honor*," Carstairs complied, making the word sound like offal.

"Mr. Caldwell, you may put on your defense." No stranger to courtrooms, Jake Tulley handled the procedures and phraseology smoothly.

"Call Lem Carter and Joe Kennedy."

"One at a time, please," Tulley snapped.

"If you say so, Jake . . . er, yer honor. Lem Carter, then."

Quickly Ezekial took Lem through a patently invented story about how the miner had threatened all three with his Winchester. How they had at first

48

agreed to leave his claim, then, when their backs had been turned, the old man had tried to gun them down.

"Liar!" Timmy shouted.

"Put a rein on that brat's mouth, Mr. Prosecutor, or the bailiff will have to drop his drawers and whup his ass raw," Tulley demanded.

"Be careful, Timmy," Carstairs murmured into the boy's ear. "All our lives are at stake now. Later . . . we'll find some way to get even."

Revenge took the place of stricken grief in Timmy's eyes and they glowed with anticipation.

"Any questions?" Ezekial addressed to Carstairs.

Bart stepped forward. "I think the boy's right. You're a liar, Lem Carter. What really happened up at Benson's mine?"

Carter put on a hurt expression. "Would I lie to you?" he whined in a thick Southern accent. "I've never told a lie in my life. This miner, Benson, he tried to back-shoot us."

"Really?" Carstairs countered, sarcasm dripping from the word.

"Trust me. It's the truth, so help me, God."

"Oh? Just how well are you acquainted with God, Mr. Carter?"

"Why . . . why . . ." He turned to Jake Tulley. "Do I have to answer that one, Jake?"

"Go ahead. It won't do any harm."

"Uh . . . I've been to the tent shows, the revivals. I've been born again. Several times," he added as a hopeful afterthought. Some of his fellow hardcases snickered.

"Then you are acquainted with what God does to liars? You know the punishment set aside for perjurers? If you are born again and we can truly trust you, you know the fate that awaits those who bear

49

false witness. So, answer me again. What really happened up at the Benson mine?"

"I . . . ah, it's like I said. Linc he's mighty fast and when that ol' bas . . . fool swung up the Winchester, he sorta beat him out, that's all."

"Next witness," Tulley ordered.

Joe Kennedy told substantially the same story. When he concluded, Carstairs stalked up to him, arms behind his back.

"If I called you a liar, what would you do?"

"I'd probably shoot you down like the dog you are."

"Oh-ho! Perhaps Mr. Kennedy isn't born again?" The lounging outlaws giggled. When they subsided, Carstairs went on. "Benson had a rifle?"

"Yes, he did."

"He threatened you three tough men with it?"

"Yes he did."

"Then why didn't you take it away from him? After all three against one, that should have been easy. Why didn't you take the rifle away from him and beat him up right proper as an object lesson?"

"We did. We whomped the hell outta him first."

"Ah-ha! Then the boy, Timmy, told the truth. His father was beaten, then shot. Perhaps he told the truth in everything?"

"No! No, it wasn't that way at all. We never laid a finger on Benson. He waved that Winchester at us and Linc . . . just had to shoot him. That's all."

Carstairs made a brief summary to the mock jury, Ezekial made none. The six road agents muttered together for a few seconds, grinning and darting glances at Linc Bascomb. Then they turned around.

"Your honor, we have reached a verdict."

"What is your verdict," Tulley inquired.

"We find Linc Bascomb not guilty of the charge of murder. We find he acted in self defense. And he's gotta buy the drinks."

"You are not guilty, Mr. Bascomb. This court is adjourned. And, Linc buys the drinks."

Lone Wolf rode away from Grub Stake ten minutes later. He choked on his fury and bitterness over the depravity of some white men and the weakness of others. How glad he was he had experienced ten years with the Crow. The white man's ways were not his own. He cast off his sour mood and kneed his mount into a fast trot. He had a lot of ground to cover to Becky's camp.

FIVE

"That coffee sure smells good," Lone Wolf remarked from the edge of the clearing. "There's nothin' better, first thing in the morning."

Rebecca Caldwell concealed a secret, satisfied smile. Although her white warrior companion had done his best to sneak up on the camp and thus get one over on her, she had not been taken by surprise. "I started it when I first heard you. It should be ready by now," she teased.

"Good," he offered with a grunt. "I have quite a lot of bad news for you. A cup of Arbuckles will help it go down better."

"What is it, Lone Wolf? Are Tulley and Uncle Ezekial in Grub Stake?"

"That they are. You were right about Tulley rebuilding his gang. They're all there, close to thirty of the worst scum on the frontier. They are murdering miners, jumping claims, robbing others and generally terrorizing the town. Most people seem afraid of Tulley's men and I don't blame them. That many guns is a lot for peaceable people to face. They need help."

"Our kind of help?" Rebecca asked anxiously.

Lone Wolf thought a moment, sipping the scalding boiled coffee from a granitized tin cup. "More like a U.S. Marshal and a posse, or troops, since Colorado is a Territory."

Rebecca's disappointment showed plainly. "Isn't there some way we can get involved?"

"I didn't say there wasn't. Only, when the time comes, we will have to have reinforcements."

"What's the layout of the town?"

"There's one main street, it comes in from the south, from Silver Creek—or Denver, if you prefer it—runs for three blocks and turns east. At the central corner is a big saloon, the Mother Lode. Used to be owned by a man named Peterson."

"Used to?"

"Yeah. From what I heard, Tulley had him gunned down on his doorstep and took over. Your Uncle Ezekial runs the place. It's sort of a headquarters for Tulley and recreation for his owlhoots. There's a couple of back streets, in the southeast part of town. Mostly tents, a couple of sod houses and three nice, permanent looking clapboard and brick homes. This Peterson lived in the biggest one. Now that's empty. There's one big operating mine, the Lucky Strike, and a smelting foundry, where they get the gold and silver out of the ore. From talk I heard, Tulley plans to take over the smelter, and all that comes from it."

"We can't let him get away with that."

"No. It would mean millions for him and Roger Styles."

"With that kind of money, they could . . . they could become untouchable. Above the law."

Lone Wolf scowled. "How do you mean that?"

"We've both seen enough of how justice functions out here," Rebecca reasoned. "Those with money buy the law. They support and elect the judges, hire the sheriffs, pay the marshals. A poor man hasn't a chance. It's not . . . like Indian justice. Harsh as it is, any man has a right to face his accuser in open combat. The winner decides the right of the issue. If the one making a decision is beholden to a rich man for his position, naturally he's going to view his benefactor's case more favorably than someone unknown and on his own. Not that they . . . deliberately *twist* the law. They only bend it a little, unconsciously, in favor of those who have done them favors. Even so, white man's justice is awfully unfair."

"That's quite a speech," Lone Wolf observed dryly. "Are you saying you would prefer to return to the Oglala way?"

His barb struck home. Did she? She preferred Indian clothing, buffalo to beef or pork, and now she'd come out for the Indian way of justice. What was it she really wanted?

For a second, Rebecca's heart felt a pang of torment for the long months of agonizing work, humiliation, prejudice and loneliness. Could she, would she, go back to that?

"No. At least not until we deal with Tulley and his gang. I won't rest until all of them are in their graves."

"Not even jail?"

"We've been over this before. Those who brought my mother a premature death, first of the spirit and then of the body—though indirectly—and me five long years of horror and misery, are going to die. I promised myself that and my mother's spirit as well. The others . . . I don't care about them, unless they get in my way."

Rebecca's unrelenting vehemence sent a chill along Lone Wolf's spine. He sought to change the subject. "There are some people who are standing up to Tulley. A few at least. One of them is a man named Bart Carstairs. If we could form an alliance with them . . . ?" he let the suggestion hang.

"Of course! I should have seen that right off. We'll

do it, Lone Wolf. We'll go to Grub Stake, form a, ah, vigilance committee or something like it and drive the outlaws out. Oh, I killed two of Tulley's recruits last night."

Instantly concerned, Lone Wolf leaned forward, the crackle of the cook fire and trill of morning birds providing a bizarre underlining to Rebecca's calm announcement. "What? How?" he blurted out.

"They rode into my camp while I was, uh, bathing in the creek. I slipped up and eavesdropped. They mentioned Tulley and talked about joining him. They also wanted . . . ah, whoever it was camping there alone. They'd prowled my things and knew I was a woman. So, I showed myself, they got nasty and I shot them. We'll have some bacon and beans and then we ought to pile some stones on the bodies."

"We could detour through another town. Those kind are always wanted for one thing or another. We could use the money their bounties would bring."

"Yes, I know." Rebecca touched her beaded bag, feeling the large roll of bills she had obtained from a penitent Orville Styles, evil Roger's father, and from the bounties on the hardcases they had killed and turned in during her first encounter with the Tulley gang. It meant security. It also reminded her of a means of earning necessary money to continue her trail of vengeance. "From what you've said, though, there isn't all that much time. Let's let it go this time. We'll eat and break camp."

"Whatever you say."

Pale morning sunlight filtered through the pine needles early the next day as Rebecca and Lone Wolf watched five men, led by Joe Kennedy, leave the hotel half a block from the Mother Lode and begin their

55

day's rounds. Only their swagger and the well-tended six-shooters they carried marked them as part of any organization. Their clothing differed wildly with individual tastes and they came short and tall, cadaverously thin and beer barrel rotund. The enforcer squad made its first stop at the general store.

After they entered, only a minute passed before a querulous voice raised in protest. "What do you mean twenty percent and you get a look at my books? I own this business and I say who sees what."

"Not any more you don't," Joe Kennedy growled.

"Now see here. Those books are private."

"Sure," Kennedy offered easily. "An' unless you pay your twenty percent and do as you're told, they'll be the private property of the new owner, Jake Tulley."

"New . . . ?"

"Mr. Tulley likes to keep the peace, have things run smooth-like. That costs money. It's up to you merchants to provide that money. So you pay and behave and you get to keep your store here. Otherwise . . . well, accidents do happen."

"Th-that's a threat."

"No, it's not. It's a promise."

The bell on the worn wooden cash drawer tinkled. "I . . . I've only taken in thirty-five dollars this week, cash money. All the rest is charge."

"You pay twenty percent on charges, too."

"But that would break me. I haven't even been paid as yet. I can't tolerate that!"

Listening outside, Rebecca and Lone Wolf heard the solid smack of a fist on flesh. "You want to keep them teeth, storeman and you'll pay up right on the dot. Every Wednesday is your day. We'll be back for more later."

Breakfast followed for the bandits. The vengeance seeking pair waited out of sight until the hardcases showed on the street once more. Tulley's men went to the livery and took out their horses. Rebecca and Lone Wolf ran to get their own.

A ten minute ride brought Kennedy's collectors to the first small mining claim. Without dismounting, the hard-faced, squat-framed Irish outlaw extended a hand in demand.

"Sorry, Mr. Kennedy," the claim owner began. "We didn't hit a hint of color this week. Nothin'."

"That's not what the assay office said, Turner. Way we figure it, you owe Mr. Tulley the sum of eighteen dollars. You can pay in dust or nuggets or in cash money."

"But I don't have it, don't you see? I . . . I'm willing to be reasonable, but in order to make anything at all, I have to have supplies, food all that sort of thing. I spent the little we brought in."

"Then that's your grief, ain't it, Turner. Next week your donation will be double."

"Why, why that's impossible. It will leave me with nothing at all."

"Shoulda thought of that before you twiddled away what you made this week." A well-worn Colt appeared in Kennedy's fist. He jumped his horse three steps closer to the quailing miner and whipped downward with the hard steel barrel of his six-gun.

The blow raked along the side of Turner's head and he fell with a groan, curled into a tight ball of misery and unconsciousness. Kennedy signed to his men and they rode on.

In rapid succession, five more claims were visited and "contributions" taken from the weaker miners who had knuckled under to Tulley's extortion. Rebecca made careful note of every cent collected. Lone Wolf could see the seething anger rising within the girl and knew she would not long tolerate this high-handed action by Tulley's gunmen.

At last, the gunslicks reached a small farmstead several miles from the ore-laden ridge where men toiled to wrest the precious metals from the ground. They skulked through the underbrush until they had the place surrounded, then moved in like a band of attacking Arapaho. With whoops and hollers they descended on the defenseless homesteader and his family. The man, caught in the open, was clubbed down and his screaming wife struggled to close the door, to no avail.

Lone Wolf reached out and restrained Rebecca from drawing her Smith & Wesson. "Not now. We have to pick the time and place."

She smiled warmly at him. He, too, she realized had no doubt that but eventually they would fall on these evil scavengers. It heartened her.

"Why are you doing this?" the farmwife wailed while Tulley's men dragged her and three small children from the sod and log dwelling.

"You an' yer old man 'uv been spreading tales about Mr. Tulley. He wants it stopped. You refused to pay up your contribution to the general welfare like honest folks. Worse, you done urged others not to pay. You're like pisen in these parts. So, by order of Marshal Tulley, you have got to go," Kennedy told her, reciting as from rote. He waved an arm to encompass the outbuildings and the house.

"Burn it all, boys. Leave 'em two horses to ride out on. Better than they deserve, sure and that's the truth."

"No!" the distraught woman shrieked. "We've worked so hard. Please, no."

"Make it good, boys. Mr. Tulley don't want one stick atop another."

With a pitiful sob, the homesteader dropped to her

knees beside her unconscious husband. She enfolded her children in her outstretched arms and wept with them as the outlaws destroyed their future and their dreams.

On the hillside above, Rebecca Caldwell restrained her fury from an unplanned attack, though she soundly and colorfully cursed the bandits and the vile man who led them.

"All right, lads," Joe Kennedy summoned his brigands. "We've got them other miners to visit, yet. Let's light a shuck."

The small placer operation worked smoothly. Ed Daws and his three partners had mined together through the Silver Creek boom, the Cripple Creek bonanza and two high color strikes in the mountains north of Santa Fe. Each knew his job and did it well. Their peaceful routine seemed idyllic, until two gunshots shattered the still morning air. The men dropped their tools and ran for their weapons.

"We warned you to sell this claim, Daws," Joe Kennedy yelled from the trees. "Now you're gonna die on it. Let's hit 'em, lads!"

The outlaws swarmed down onto the confused miners, Winchesters and six-guns blazing. Behind them, Rebecca pointed to a screened position half way down the curving slope of the small creek-side claim. Lone Wolf nodded his agreement. An ideal place from which to employ his sturdy war bow and the Spencer he carried in his saddle scabbard.

"Now we get them, Lone Wolf. Now they pay."

SIX

At first, Joe Kennedy thought the miners had managed to rally and offer effective resistance. Then he realized that Nate Williams had been shot from behind. Someone, from outside the small claim site had thrown in their hand. He whirled in time to see a woman riding down on them. No, not a woman, his mind worked out, a squaw. A . . . *white* squaw.

She wore a bead-decorated Sioux squaw dress and high moccasins, her hair in braids. And, he added a moment before he saw the muzzle bloom, she held a revolver in her right hand.

Then the thirty-eight slug sped toward him and ripped into his left shoulder. The pain screamed at him and he bent sideways, the Remington in his right hand momentarily forgotten.

Rebecca raced down on him, her finger already tightening on the trigger for a second shot. Accurate fire from horseback was a chancy proposition under any circumstances. When her first round went wide, Rebecca wasted no time in regret. She automatically adjusted her point of aim and fired again.

Joseph Kennedy's face took on an expression of utter astonishment when the slug struck him high in the chest, a fraction of an inch below the gullcy formed by his collar bones. The soft lead bullet lost little of its shape, a blunt cone that slammed solidly into his spine and shattered the vital nerves that

60

controlled his body. Involuntarily, he leaped into the air like a jumping jack and fell back to earth in a twitching heap.

The gunmen with him looked up in confused disbelief at the awesome image of the vengeful woman who charged down on them. One of the outlaws shrieked and spun to one side, his body transfixed by an arrow, the gore-smeared flint head protruding from his chest.

"Christ and all the saints!" a hardcase gusted out, the closest to prayer he had been since childhood. "Wha . . ."

His voice cut off in a bubble of blood when a second feathered shaft pierced his throat. The remaining three bandits started to run.

Ed Daws blasted the life out of one Tulley man with his big Sharps 50-140-800. The gunhawk seemed to float upward into the air, legs still churning in obedience to the last command of his dying brain. The heavy roar of another Sharps sounded from among the rocks where Lone Wolf provided covering fire.

Rebecca swung her Baby Russian toward another hardcase and blasted away a bit of his right ear, setting off a shower of blood spray. He threw down the Winchester he had held and dropped to his knees.

"No-no! Don't shoot. I give up," he wailed.

The remaining outlaw decided to make a fight of it.

His odds, never good to begin with, ran out when Rebecca's Ike smashed into him and she lowered her arm until the gunslick stared into the muzzle of the .38 Smith & Wesson. At such short range, he never saw the fat bloom of fire that followed the departure of the slug that shattered his brain. Quickly, Rebecca dismounted and ran to the outlaw who had surrendered.

"Give me a reason not to kill you," she coolly told him.

"I . . . I ain't armed. I done gave up."

"That'll do for now."

Lone Wolf trotted down from the rocks, leading his horse. He stopped beside Rebecca a moment before the rescued miners swarmed around.

"You're some surprise, lady," Ed Daws proclaimed. "But none could be more welcome. You an' your, uh, friend here saved our lives. We're beholden."

"Uh, yeah. Thank you," Ed's partners mumbled together, their attention captured by Lone Wolf's blond roach hairstyle and Crow warrior's clothing.

"Ah, no offense, but, er, with those arrows and your, ah, clothes . . ." Ed stammered.

"We were both captives of the Indians," Rebecca explained with accustomed ease, used to the remarks of whites. "Long enough to get to like the comfortable clothing."

"If you're fightin' Jake Tulley and his gang, it wouldn't matter if you was stark nekkid," Pete Lewis exclaimed.

"I'll accept that as approval," Rebecca told him, a light pink tinge in her cheeks. "Now, there are a few questions to ask this one."

"I ain't sayin' nothin'," the outlaw muttered.

"Oh, I think you will. What's Tulley's reason for coming to Grub Stake?"

The hardcase glowered at Rebecca. He wasn't about to answer any questions from a woman, he told himself. His fear of death gone, he crossed his arms over his chest in defiance and remained silent.

"Lone Wolf, how did the Crow handle a prisoner who wouldn't talk?"

"Oh, sometimes they would shove his hand in a fire, hold it until the skin peeled. Or they would slice little strips of hide off him until he opened up. They had lots of ways."

"Start a fire," Rebecca commanded.

"You can't . . . it ain't civilized," the cowering gunman protested in vain.

"Make it a little one," the woman standing over him suggested. "There was a warrior in Iron Calf's band who had traveled far to the south. He used to tell about the things he'd seen the Apaches do. How they would build a tiny fire of twigs on a man's belly and roast him open. Or put one between his legs and cook his balls."

The gunhawk cringed. Blood still flowed from his damaged ear. "Not that! Please, don't do that to me," he begged.

"What is your name?" Rebecca demanded.

"Kerwin. Dave Kerwin."

"Well, Dave, we'd like to know all about Jake Tulley. What is he up to?"

"I . . . I can't tell you. He'd have my hide if I did."

"And we have it now."

Lone Wolf reached down and ripped open Kerwin's shirt. He drew his long, wide-bladed hunting knife and swiftly drew a shallow slit across the badman's chest.

Kerwin screamed.

"Yes," Rebecca managed to say calmly. "I think skinning him might be interesting. Let me make the next cut."

"That . . . that's heathen," Ed Daws protested.

"He and his friends were trying to kill you."

"Sure. And I'd like to see him hang for it. But this . . . it goes again' the grain."

Rebecca didn't make answer. She holstered her revolver and drew her skinning knife from the sheath on the cartridge belt she now wore around her waist.

Dave Kerwin eyed it and began to babble.

"I-I-I-I'll talk. I'll tell you everything you want to know. Just . . . don't . . . use that . . . knife."

With deft questioning by Rebecca and Lone Wolf, Kerwin detailed Tulley's plan for taking and holding Grub Stake and revealed that Roger Styles had summoned the outlaw leader there. He knew only a part of the whole scheme, but enough to indicate Roger's political ambitions and that the mastermind behind the Bitter Creek Jake gang was in Denver. So astonishing was his story that his interrogators gave it total concentration. Dave Kerwin took quick advantage of this.

His hand darted out toward the Smith & Wesson in Rebecca's holster. She jumped back, though not before his fingers closed over the polished walnut grips and jerked the weapon free. Then Lone Wolf shot him at extreme close range with his big Sharps.

Kerwin's head swelled like a hot air balloon, then exploded into hundreds of gory pieces. His body flopped on the ground like a landed fish and blood sprayed from the shattered remains of his skull, the lower jaw exposed to give them a skeletal grin.

"My God! Oh, my God!" Ed Dawes exclaimed. He turned away and vomited with violent retches.

"He gave us everything he knew, I'm sure of that," Rebecca told Lone Wolf after she overcame her own queasy reaction to the sudden killing. "Which means we have some planning to do."

"Yes. He could have lived," Lone Wolf observed. "If only he hadn't made a play for your revolver."

"It's over now." Rebecca addressed her words to the three miners. "Bury these bodies somewhere out of sight and chase off their horses. If Tulley or any of his men came around asking, you never saw them and don't know anything."

"Yes, Ma'am," Pete Lewis gulped.

A twenty minute ride from the scene of the shootout, Rebecca and Lone Wolf halted in a clearing. "Lone Wolf, I want you to ride to Denver. We need help to stop Tulley. Get the U.S. Marshal."

"Why don't you do that, while I keep an eye on what is going on in Grub Stake?"

"Meaning it would be safer that way? No. Politics and the law are man's doings. I wouldn't be listened to half so seriously as you. You should wear white man's clothing, to save a lot of explaining. Also, it would be wise to shave off that roach. You could be taken for a renegade. There has been trouble with a man named Chivington, who seems determined to start an Indian war, and you can't be too careful."

Lone Wolf scowled, his lips pushed out into a dour expression. "I'll cut my hair. But white man's clothes are tight and uncomfortable. I . . . oh, you're right I suppose. I can leave any time."

"Do it now."

SEVEN

From a stand of tall pines, Rebecca Caldwell looked down on the one-man mining operation. The musical *clang-scrape-clang* of a single-jack drill rose on the early morning air. Wispy fragments of cloud tore apart on the needle-clustered boughs above her head and for once she was appreciative of the extra warmth of white woman's clothes.

Rebecca wore her maroon riding habit and English boots, her hair loose and swept upward in a thick cascade that nearly hid the small velvet hat with its perky feather. Around her waist she had belted the holster that held her Baby Russian. She felt confined, though grateful that the heavy cloth and many layers of material sheltered her from the chill breeze. The drill song stopped and a burly man, the red sleeves of his longjohns showing from rolling up shirtsleeves, appeared at the low opening into the rock of the hillside.

"Fire in the hole!" he yelled, not any too loudly. The miner had a full beard, streaked with gray splotches of rock dust, thick shoulders and long arms that ended in ham-like hands. He seemed to scuttle across the ground, small puffs rising from the heels of his boots. He went to a tall, sturdy mule and held its muzzle. A minute passed in absolute quiet.

Then Rebecca felt a thump and roll through the ground, followed by the muffled boom of an explosion

66

and the subterranean rattle of falling rock. A billow of smoke and dust boiled out of the mine entrance. While the man waited for that to clear, Rebecca rode downhill toward him.

"Hello, the mine!" she called out, mindful of the touchy nature of those around Grub Stake.

The miner reached for the Winchester, propped against a tree near where he stood. Intelligent brown eyes sparkled in the grime-smeared face. "Hello, yerself." Then his brows shot upward when he recognized the visitor to be a woman.

"What'er you doin' out this way, Missy?"

"I have been talking with some people who aren't particularly pleased with Jake Tulley and his gang. They said I should speak to you. You are Mike Hoxsey? Hard Rock Mike?"

The miner knocked dust from his clothes and smoothed a hand over his beard. "That's me. Who might you be?"

"My name is Rebecca Caldwell. I have even more reason to detest Jake Tulley than you people. Five years worth of reasons."

"I think I could rustle up some coffee," Hoxsey offered.

"That would be lovely," Rebecca returned.

While he worked around a small fire, fiddling with the granite pot and a pound bag of Arbuckles, Mike studied the girl. Some looker, young, too, he mused. Has a sort of Injun cast to her eyes and cheekbones, he observed. Suddenly, something he had heard registered. His brows arched and he saw her in a new light.

"Say, you wouldn't happen to be the gal who did for some of Tulley's men yesterday, would you?"

"I am. My uncle, Ezekial Caldwell, rides with Tulley. A little over five years ago, they traded my mother and I to the Sioux in exchange for their own worthless lives."

"Glory be! Then . . . then you'd be the one that rumor has it is huntin' Tulley down. Ran him outta Nebraska, was it?"

"Sort of," Rebecca admitted, cautious of a sudden. "W-what else have you heard?"

"Uh . . . that you an' some white Injun shot hell outta Tulley's gang, including one of your blood relation."

"Yes. Uncle Virgil. I'm not going to stop until they all pay for what they did to us."

"Then, Missy Caldwell, you found the right people to help. Have you been to talk with Bart Carstairs yet?"

"No, I haven't. Who is he?"

"He was gonna be our mayor until Tulley moved in. Look, I'll set up a meetin' of some of the folks most willin' to do something about Tulley. Carstairs, Katie O'Day, young Matthew Peterson. For . . . say, tonight, after the town settles down a bit?"

"That would be fine, Mr. Hoxsey."

Hard Rock Mike wiped dust from a tin cup and poured from the boiling pot. "Call me Mike. An' here's your coffee."

"Oh, thank you." Rebecca took it and cupped the vessel in both hands, enjoying the warmth that spread up her arms from her clasped fingers. "Is it always this cold of a morning?"

"Yep. At least here in the Rockies. Worse in winter. But I figure to get me enough of a stake to spend the bad months further south. Say in Matamoros, over in Ol' Mexico. That suits my old bones much better, Miss Caldwell."

"Oh, if I'm to call you Mike, please call me Rebecca."

"Rebecca . . . Becky . . . that's a right purty name. I used to have a daughter by that name. Lost her in the cholera epidemic back East in the winter of Fifty-six. M'wife, too."

"I am sorry to hear that," Rebecca offered automatically.

Hard Rock Mike shrugged. "My boys were mostly growed, so we headed West. Turned out to be the best thing ever happened to all of us. One boy's runnin' cattle down in Texas. Rode with Hood's division in the War Between the States. The other's a barber in Dodge City. Me . . . I'm doin' what I like most."

"You don't look old enough to have grown children, Mike."

"Uh . . . I eat lots of buffalo and bear, Becky. Keeps a feller young lookin'. My oldest went to war as a drummer boy, only twelve at the time. The other's barely nineteen now."

"Mummm. This is good coffee, Mike."

"Self defense. If you're gonna cook for yourself, you might as well do it right, I figure."

"You have a good point. I'm afraid I'm keeping you from your work." She started to rise.

"Ain't had this pleasant an interruption in a long time. Tonight, then? Say, about ten or so?"

"Where?"

"In the back room of Katie's Silver Creek Cafe."

"Good enough for me."

"You take care of yourself, now, y'hear?"

Rebecca gave him a warm, sincere smile. "Oh, I will, Mike, I surely will."

Ty Purdy sat on the spring seat of his buckboard, staring disconsolately at the smoldering embers of his house and barn. His wife, Grace, sat beside him, a

69

small lace hankie fighting unsuccessfully to stem the tide of tears that rolled down her plump cheeks. Behind them, in the nearly empty wagon box, three tow-headed youngsters peered over the sides. The eldest, a boy, wore a solemn, wide-eyed expression. The other two sniffled and battled their own salty flows. Rebecca found them like that, amid the ruins of their homestead.

"I'm sorry Tulley's men destroyed your place yesterday," she began after the introductions. "What was the reason?"

"He . . . he expected a share of fifty-percent of my crop, if I ever got one, in exchange for what his men called 'protection.' Damned if I was gonna take that. Weren't never a sharecropper and didn't intend to be one on my own land. I shoulda gunned them all down."

"You were wise not to resist alone, Mr. Purdy. Tulley's outlaws are all hardened killers, totally ruthless. They . . ." Rebecca lowered her voice slightly. "They would not have spared your wife and children."

"I know the sort. Where do you figure into all of this?"

Rebecca explained for what she thought must be the hundredth time about her captivity among the Sioux. "So I have determined to hunt down those responsible and see that justice is done."

Ty Purdy shrugged. "What would the courts do? Those that ain't for sale to the highest bidder would consider it your word against all of theirs."

For a moment, Rebecca's lips formed a grim, determined line, then she spoke, exposing neat, even white teeth. "I don't intend to take them to court, Mr. Purdy."

Purdy eyed the Smith & Wesson strapped to her waist. "Uh . . . yes. You're a brave woman, Miss

Caldwell. What did you come to me for?"

"I thought you might want a chance to get even."

Anger glowed deep in Ty Purdy's eyes. Yes, it would be good to give those hardcases a little of their own medicine. He glanced at his wife. She had paled at Rebecca's mention of a more direct form of revenge than lawmen and courtrooms. Now her lower lip quivered and she sought the words to convince her husband to let it all lie, to pull stakes and find a new place. Before she could speak, Purdy put a work-callused hand over hers.

"A man's got to stand up eventually, Grace. If he's any sort of a man. Tulley's a criminal, one of the worst kind. If everyone turns their backs, no tellin' what awful thing he will do next."

"But . . . why you, Ty?" his wife returned in a small voice. "You're not a gunhand. Why, outside of hunting for meat, you never use your gun."

"I fought with Grant's army. Appears we did all right. Besides, what sort of example is that for Tommy an' Jamie, or even little Jenny? Always knuckling under, running away from trouble." He pointed to Rebecca. "Why, look at her. She's a woman an' she's willin' to fight Tulley."

Grace Purdy's eyes narrowed disapprovingly. "Yes. But she . . . she's . . ."

"Lived with the Sioux? Yes, I did. I learned how to use a rifle and a knife and a bow. Not because I wanted to, but because I had to to survive. Killing a man is not all that much more difficult than killing a deer, Mrs. Purdy. I don't consider Jake Tulley and his gang to be all that human. Even the Oglala killed rabid animals. I'm going to fight Jake Tulley in Grub Stake, with or without your husband's help."

Ty Purdy's bleak stare shut off further protest from his wife. "You can count on me, Miss Caldwell. I'll need to find a safe place for m'wife and kids first, though."

"Do that. Can you be back to Grub Stake by ten tonight?"

"I reckon I can."

"There will be a meeting at the Silver Creek Cafe at that time. Join us and we can lay plans."

From her place of hiding in a low wash outside Grub Stake Rebecca watched the activity in the small boomtown. Tulley's gunhawks walked the streets with the swagger of bullies, while the locals, miners, trappers and few homesteaders moved about with their heads ducked, furtively, as though expecting a blow. Business appeared to go on as usual, though silence hung, pall-like over the streets. Lone Wolf was right, she thought. Even though Tulley had been in town less than a week, his evil had pervaded every part of life in Grub Stake.

Rebecca returned to her surveillance. Twice she noticed a particularly handsome young man, of perhaps twenty-two or three, with soft blond hair that blew in the wind, a slim body, wearing a gray suit, no hat and brightly polished boots on small feet. He seemed to be about five-foot nine and people spoke to him deferentially, as though to a person of respect and power, or to one recently bereaved. His gentle, ready smile, twinkling blue eyes and feline grace caused a stirring in her loins. She made note of him, wondering who he might be. A loud whoop, from the direction of the Mother Lode saloon, caught her attention and she directed her gaze there.

Three of Tulley's gunhawks, reeling drunk, staggered out into the street. With them they brought an unkempt, whiskered little man with a battered bowler hat and tattered frock coat, its black cloth rumpled and dust-covered.

"Mr. Tulley don't want trash like you in his place, rummy."

"Awh, please, Mr. Morton. I was . . . I was only tryin to . . . to rustle up a little eye-opener. The times has been hard on me, that's all. Y-you unnerstand, don' you, Mr. Morton?"

The blond, scraggly-haired killer gave the old man a shove that nearly sent him off his feet. "Get along, you old bag of shit. Go cadge drinks somewhere else."

"Hey, Clyde," one of the gunslingers shouted. "Le's see iffin he can dance? Huh? What say?" He already had his six-gun out.

A wild glint came to Morton's eyes. "Sure, why not?" His hand blurred when he dipped for the pearl-handled iron at his hip.

Two slugs spurted dust from the street near one of the old drunk's boot heels. "Owie! Don't do that, fellers. Please don't. Oh-oh-oh!" he shouted as more bullets thudded into dirt near his rapidly moving feet. When he started to run, the trio turned back laughing, to the saloon. No one, Rebecca noted, had raised a hand in defense of the helpless old man. Those closest had actually turned away to avoid involvement.

Near to supper time, a loud cheer rose from in front of the Mother Lode. A gaudily painted carriage rolled up, followed by a large closed wagon. Anger burned hotly in Rebecca's veins when she recognized her uncle Ezekial, who stepped from the saloon, wiping his hands on an apron. He assisted a blowsy, over-dressed woman from the cabriolet and greeted her with a hug. Their voices drifted down to where the white squaw watched.

"Flora, Flora, you've not changed a bit. Welcome to Grub Stake. This here's my place, the Mother Lode."

"Ugly as ever, you sumbitch," Flora Belle Chase cawed in a rough whiskey tenor. "What did you do to your arm, Ezekial?"

"I'll tell you later. That your girls?" He gestured toward the other conveyance.

"Sure is." Flora Belle raised her crow's screech to a bellow. "All right, girls. Off yer duffs and on yer feet. We've a night's work ahead of us."

When the first soiled dove stepped down the folding stairs at the rear of the wooden-sided wagon, another ragged cheer went up from the assembled miners and saloon hangers-on. Then another appeared, followed rapidly by six more. A holiday atmosphere seemed to capture the crowd.

"What'cha doin' here, lady?"

Rebecca turned to see two small, barefoot boys staring at her. They wore identical red suspenders and their flannel shirts were unbuttoned down to the waist of their linsey-woolsey trousers. The dark-haired one rubbed a big toe over a red flea bite on his other ankle.

"I'm, uh, just watching."

The tow-head spoke again. "You come with them other painted ladies?"

"No. Of course not. Shouldn't you two be at home to supper?"

"Uh . . . yeah. I s'pose so. My Maw ain't called yet."

"Mine neither," the dark one added. "See, Kelly, I tole you she weren't no fancy girl."

"Do you boys like candy?" Rebecca inquired. Instantly their eyes lighted. She extended her hand, with a ten cent piece in it. "If I give you a dime to buy

74

some will you not mention you saw me to anyone?"

"A whole dime!" the boys breathed out together. The blond, Kelly, reached out and grabbed it.

"Don't worry, lady. We didn't see a thing." They ran off giggling.

"We're all right pleased to make your acquaintance, Miss Caldwell," Kathlene O'Day spoke for the people gathered late that night in a dimly lighted room behind her cafe. "If you'll excuse me, I'll leave you to get acquainted with the others. My youngest, Kelly, ain't feelin' all so good. He didn't eat all his supper an' he's a might peaked around the gills. Sure an' I hope he ain't comin' down with something."

Oh-oh, Rebecca thought. At least she knew the identity of one of the youngsters who had sneaked up on her in the gully. She hoped his bellyache, induced by the candy she had indirectly provided, wouldn't strain relations with his mother. Right now, though, her main concern was the terribly handsome young man she had seen earlier in the day. He sat next to her, acutely aware of her presence.

"Matthew Peterson. It was your father's saloon that Tulley took over, right?"

"Yes, the murdering bas—swine. I'll get even if it's the last thing I do."

"Mike Hoxsey, over there, suggested I talk with you."

"Hummm. I'm glad he did." His eyes revealed that he had more in mind than revenge. He frankly examined Rebecca, conscious of the heady aura of womanliness about her, his youthful juices running hot and powerful through him. Her raven hair and stark blue eyes contrasted nicely with the golden skin and high cheek bones. She carried herself well, though

75

seemingly unfamiliar with women's clothing. He had caught a glimpse of her horse and knew she didn't ride sidesaddle. The prospect excited him.

Ever since he'd been a little pecker-puller of eight or so he had heard tales from his friends and older boys about how horny girls were who rode split-legged on their horses. The stories had made him steamy in the crotch then, now the thought made his blood percolate. His chicken-choker fantasies had first become reality one glorious spring afternoon a few weeks after his thirteenth birthday. From that time on he had pursued that marvelous, moist female cavern with single-minded determination. He wondered if Rebecca Caldwell was as much all business and revenge as she seemed to be.

"Mike's been telling us that you've been after the Tulley gang for some time now," Bart Carstairs remarked.

"A bit over two months, actually," Rebecca told him.

"And before that you were a captive of the Sioux?"

"That's right, Mr. Carstairs. In the camp of Iron Calf, the Oglala chief. Again, Jake Tulley is to blame for that. He and my low-life uncles."

"Caldwell," Ty Purdy mused. "I thought the name sounded familiar. Is . . . is Ezekial Caldwell at the Mother Lode related?"

"My uncle. He's ridden with Tulley for nearly six years."

"What about the other uncle you mentioned?" Hard Rock Mike inquired.

"He died about two weeks ago."

"Oh? Is that before you had a chance to confront Tulley and his men?" Carstairs asked.

"No. I shot Virgil Caldwell down like the dog he was."

Lord, is she that hard against all men? Matt Peterson speculated. No. He could almost smell her eager need for a man. For all her cold-bloodedness, he could sense that Rebecca was a warm and passionate woman, well developed and, he judged, well schooled in the arts of love. It made his pulse quicken even more and caused a swelling in his loins.

"Ah, there we are, chattin' like old friends at tea," Kathlene O'Day began, returning from her child's bedside. "Now, my dear, what is it you propose to do that we haven't thought of already?" she addressed to Rebecca.

"You need to organize. Those who oppose Tulley should band together to provide mutual protection. I've sent a friend to Denver for the U.S. Marshal. Until the law gets here, you should be able to protect each other from Tulley's vandals day and night."

"Ya mean put guards on all our places? Why, child, when would we ever have time for work, or sleep for that matter?"

"It's that or suffer the consequences. I've been watching Tulley's gang. You can ask Mr. Purdy here. He tried to buck them alone."

"An' lost my homestead for it, too."

"Who's this friend you mentioned?" Matt Peterson asked.

"He's called Lone Wolf."

"An Injun?"

"No, Mr. Peterson. Another captive, like myself. He lived ten years with the Crow. Says he's so used to his Indian name that Brett Baylor seems to be some stranger."

"The Crow and Sioux are enemies," Matt challenged her, sudden, unjustified jealousy fueling his suspicion.

"Right you are, Mr. Peterson. I met Lone Wolf

during a Crow raid on Iron Calf's village. He . . . helped me escape."

"I heard about that raid," Carstairs mused. "The army said no one survived."

"Not so. Since then I have discovered that thirty people managed to flee in time and have joined Spotted Elk's band north of the Black Hills."

"Did you leave, ah, anyone in the Sioux village? And, please, call me Matt."

Rebecca smiled briefly to acknowledge the familiar form of address. "No, Matt. Only my mother. She had been killed by the Crow warriors."

"Oh, you poor dear," Kathlene O'Day gushed. "So close to freedom and to have that happen. I feel so sorry for her. And for you, too, my pet."

"Thank you, Mrs. O'Day."

"Kelly heard your voice. He says it was you who gave him and Sean Corkrin the money for candy. Though, if ye were spyin' on the likes o' Jake Tulley an' his men at the time, I'll not be for holdin' that again' ye."

"Thanks again, Mrs. O'Day. I . . . never thought. All I wanted was not to attract attention. Now, back to what to do until the marshal gets here."

"Such as?" Ty Purdy inquired.

"If you can afford it, pay whatever is demanded of you. A promise made under duress isn't binding and no violation of your word. At least that's what my mother taught me."

"Outrageous!" Bart Carstairs exploded.

"No it's not," Rebecca countered. "Think of it a moment. The only ones harmed so far are those who openly showed resistance. If you seemingly go along, you will be ready to fight if necessary when the U.S. marshal arrives. I'll be back from time to time, as will Lone Wolf once he's notified the marshal. Whatever we can do, we will."

"That's all, then?" Ty Purdy asked disappointedly.

"It's a hell of a lot," Mike Hoxsey declared. "If you want my opinion, it's more than the handwringing and gripin' we've been doin' since that scoundrel got here. I say we break this up before Tulley's gunslicks get word of it. I can do a turn of watchin' until daylight. Then I got to get me some rest and protect my claim."

"I'll work out a schedule that will fit all of us," Bart offered. "It will be ready at my store tomorrow. Good night, all of you."

"Where will you be staying, uh, Rebecca?"

"I have a hidden camp a couple of miles out of town, Matt."

"Perhaps it would be best if I escorted you there . . . ah, all things considered?"

"Yes. I suppose it would."

They said their good-nights and left the cafe in silence. Now they rode along without speaking until Rebecca pointed out her small campsite. She dismounted and Matt did also.

"I . . . well, I suppose this is good night, uh, Becky." Matt took Rebecca's hand almost shyly.

"There's no need for you to hurry off, Matt. But, first, I want to get out of these uncomfortable clothes. I feel more at home in a Sioux dress."

Without another word, Rebecca removed all of her white woman's garb. Matt gaped, slack-jawed, at the thrilling beauty that stood before him in the silvery moonlight. Blood rushed to his groin and his penis came to throbbing life, rising painfully against the tightness of his trousers.

Rebecca reached casually for her elk-hide dress,

then stopped. "No. Rather than me put this on, I think it would be better for you to get out of those clothes, Matt Peterson."

Matt's heart thudded in eagerness while he hurriedly stripped. His long, thick penis swung into view. Rebecca looked at it, thrilled by anticipation of the joy it could bring. She motioned toward her bedroll.

"Y-you are a beautiful woman, Becky." He stepped close to her and she felt his swollen manhood brush lightly against the upper fringe of her sparse pubic bush. Rebecca breathed deeply and Matt put one arm around her shoulder, drawing her closer.

"You have a marvelous body, Matt," she told him sincerely. Her hand reached out and circled his pulsating cock. Little tremors of delight surged through Matt's body, followed by even more intense tingling when she began to stroke him.

"Especially this. In Sioux it is called a *sluka*, or foreskin pushed back—a man's organ as opposed to a little boy's. It's evident you're no beginner, Matt Peterson, which is all the more to the good."

His other hand found her warm, moist cleft and felt it unfold to welcome him. He slid a dexterous middle finger into the outer chamber of her golden passage and used thumb and forefinger to locate and ardently massage the swelling little button at the apex of her pleasure cave. Rebecca quivered a tremor of utter delight.

"You're not cold, are you?" Matt inquired softly, his voice solicitous. "It takes a while to get accustomed to our chill nights."

"There are some warm, soft blankets and a buffalo robe right there to shelter us. But first . . ." Rebecca sank to her knees, her body shuddering violently in the grip of her passion. She had ached with the desire for a man during the past two weeks since their murderous encounter with the Bitter Creek Jake Tulley gang. In all that time she had not seen one more ideally suited for the love combat than Matt Peterson. Quickly she bent forward to pleasure him in the manner she had learned from her second Oglala husband, Broken Wing.

One hand cupped the taut sack of his scrotum, fingers kneading the firm pebbles within, while her mobile lips nuzzled the swollen, blunt purple tip of his huge maleness. The feathery movements tickled him with an intensity that nearly merged pleasure and pain. Matt writhed and thrust his hips while Rebecca slowly engorged more of his throbbing shaft. Carefully she swallowed it, slathering the hot flesh with her tongue, lubricating it for its maximum penetration.

In he went, deeper until his sensitive head felt the muscular rings of her throat and he realized she was taking him to the root. Impossible! he thought wildly. No one had ever handled that much before. Yet, inch by inch, his foot-plus love lance disappeared into her eager, industriously working mouth. When her small, straight nose nestled in the bristly blond thatch of his pubic hair, she began to hum happily and rock back and forth on her heels.

Matt clapped both hands to the back of her head and convulsed mightily in the grip of nearly unbearable ecstasy. On and on Rebecca worked, herself transported by the pleasure it brought her to consume this sweet-tasting organ and bring such unutterable pleasure to the marvelous hunk of man she serviced.

"Becky! Aaaaah . . . B-B-Becky! It's mar . . . vel . . . ous!" Matt cried out when he could no longer contain his vital sap. His belly cramped and he exploded his nectar far down her silken throat.

Quickly Rebecca eased back, allowing her to breathe and control the warm flow that coursed out from his manhood. Their first love clash completed in mutual happiness, they sank onto the piled blankets in perspiring satisfaction.

Rebecca's questing fingers discovered that, like Four Horns so long ago, Matt had not lost his magnificent erection. She guided it downward until the tingling tip became enfolded in her lacy portals. She thrust forward with her pelvis until his massive member made contact with the opening to her slippery passage. Lubricated by the constant, heavy, warm flow of her juices, Matt slowly inserted his palpitating bulk. She groaned at the way it stretched her tunnel to the maximum, thrilled to the edge of her endurance by the contentment it brought her.

"More, Matt. Let me have it all!" she keened out.

Bright colored lights exploded behind Rebecca's eyes as Matt pressed on her, driving his great shaft to the utter limits. There he paused while Rebecca performed a hidden dance of love with the clever muscles that controlled her inner secrets. He felt himself rising to another peak and slowly began to withdraw.

"No. Don't," Rebecca begged. "Don't ever take it away."

"Only for a little bit, love," Matt crooned. He withdrew until nearly all of him felt the chill night air, then plunged in again, swifter, with the power of his muscular thighs behind it. Rebecca shrieked her delight.

Holding himself in now, Matt powered his way into Rebecca's inner being, establishing a staying rhythm that they both rocked to while time became ice-bound and the stars whirled above in their glittering constellations. Rebecca felt her own moment approaching and ground her pelvis into him, her mind swimming in enchantment, while her body hummed and vibrated to nature's oldest song. Then she lost control in the ultimate climax of her life.

"Now . . . now . . . now . . . oh, oh-oh-oh-oh *God* . . . *it's* . . . *good!*" she cried out. "Matty, Matty . . . you're soooo . . . good . . . for me!"

The wild convulsions of her explosion plumbed him to his core and Matt teetered on the edge of his own giant release. He changed stride, slowing, sending trembles of joy through both of them.

"Oh, no. No! It . . . can't . . . be . . . better than . . . that!" Rebecca cried out.

Only it was.

Matt filled her like an undulating telegraph pole, awakening sensations she had never before experienced. For himself, he had never felt more alive, yet so close to death. Each surge became a new vista of perfection for him. His belly muscles ached and he thought, time after time, that his heart would stop. Yet he drove on, Becky's nails raked his back and she sank teeth into his shoulder. The pain quickly became pleasure.

Then, after another shrieking climax from the delightful girl beneath him, Matt slowly floated up the incline to the "little death" and surged over the side in a gush of life sap.

They lay till for only a few long-ticking minutes. Again, the fine edge of Matt's phenomenal rigidity never left him. As he lay on his back, Becky straddled him and impaled her dripping purse with his iron-hard maleness. With him fully ingested, she began to grind her pouting wet mound against his pubic arch and Matt knew he wouldn't get home until at least dawn. Somehow, he thought, the grin spread wide on his face, he really didn't care.

EIGHT

He would change clothes and have his head shaved when he first reached Denver. Lone Wolf resigned himself to it, although aware of the necessity, he could already feel the discomfort. He should be there by late afternoon. He had pushed hard all the previous day, making, by his estimate, some sixty miles from Grub Stake. Then he would locate the marshal. Once back on the trail, he promised himself, he would go back to his Crow war shirt, leggings and breech cloth. The thought of boots appalled him after ten years without them. Many white men wore moccasins, he rationalized. That was one concession he would not make. A short distance ahead of him, three men rode out of the trees and blocked the trail.

"Look what we've got here, Marv. A gawdamned renegade," the one in the center announced.

"Been livin' with the Arapaho or them damned Cheyennes," Marv speculated aloud. Like his companions, he held a Winchester in his hands, the muzzle centered on Lone Wolf's body. "Lord, how I hate them Cheyenne."

"The Cheyenne's gonna get theirs, don't worry. The colonel done promised that."

"What do we do with this one, Arch? Shall we string him up?"

"Naw. The colonel wouldn't like that. We better question him first, find out what the heathen bastards are up to."

"Who are you men and what is this about a colonel?" Lone Wolf demanded, uneasy at the presence of weapons, yet determined not to show any weakness.

"He speaks American right well, don't he?" Archie Mills sneered. "That'll make questionin' him easier. What's yer name, renegade?"

"My name is Lone . . . uh, Brett Baylor and I am not a renegade."

"Lone what was that?"

"I was a captive of the Crow. They called me Lone Wolf."

"Crow my ass! You're in cahoots with them sneakin', murderin' Cheyennes," Marv snapped. He jabbed his arm forward and poked the muzzle of his rifle into Lone Wolf's ribs.

Archie put a restraining hand on his subordinate's arm. "Take it easy, Marv. Could be he's been with the Arapaho, with that funny hair-do." His mood changed. "You might as well know who it is got you, renegade. I'm Sergeant Mills and these are Privates Jones and Marsh, Colonel Chivington's Colorado Volunteers. The old man heard rumors that the Cheyenne were fixin' to get up a raid on Silver Creek. You wouldn't happen to be scoutin' for them, would you?"

"Definitely not." Mention of the rag-tag "citizens' army" chilled Lone Wolf. Not six months old, they had already earned a reputation as "Indian fighters." Word on the frontier had it that their exploits consisted mostly of shooting up a few peaceful Arapaho villages. This knowledge urged him to caution.

"I've ridden this trail for sixty miles," he told his captors. "No sign of any Cheyenne in that distance."

"He's lyin'!" Marv Jones snapped.

"Of course he is. Renegades always lie," Steve Marsh added. "Let's haul him offen that horse and get the truth."

"You've got a good idea, for once," Archie said, sighing.

Quickly the two privates dismounted and dragged Lone Wolf from his saddle. In silence, five more men appeared from alongside the trail. Lone Wolf's hope of easy escape faded.

"Tie him to that tree over there, standin' up," Archie commanded. "Then someone bring me a bucket of cold water from the crick."

"That works better at night," Lone Wolf observed to Archie while the Volunteers roughly tied him to a slender pine. "Wintertime is even better."

"Watch your lip," Archie growled. 'You're in enough trouble now." He stepped closer to their captive and grabbed Lone Wolf by the jaw, twisting his head in a powerful grip.

"Now, renegade . . ."

"I'm not a renegade. My name is Brett Baylor," Lone Wolf forced out.

"Then *Mister* Baylor, suppose you answer some questions." With a sudden violent jerk, Archie released Lone Wolf's jaw. "How far away are the Cheyenne?"

"I don't know. I've not seen any Cheyenne."

"Keep on lying and you're gonna get hurt."

"I'm not lying. I was on my way to Denver . . ."

"Silver Creek," Archie snarled.

"Silver Creek, then. I have a message for the U.S. Marshal."

"In a pig's ass!" Marv fired back as he approached with a dripping leather bucket.

"Douse him," Archie ordered.

Chill Rocky Mountain water splashed on Lone Wolf's face and chest. An involuntary gasp escaped, which he quickly turned into a chuckle. "Thanks. The trail dust was gettin' a mite thick."

"You'll laugh outten the other side of your head when I get through with you. If you don't know anything about the Cheyenne, then you must be part of an Arapaho raiding party. Where are they?"

"Listen closely, Sergeant Mills. I am not a Cheyenne scout and I'm not part of an Arapaho raiding party."

"That's a war shirt yer wearin'," the Colorado Volunteer sergeant challenged.

"Yes. But it's Crow. The Crow are two hundred miles from here. They are not raiding into Colorado, and if they were it would be against the Arapaho."

"If yer a Crow warrior, why ain't you with the Crow?"

"A little matter of killing a war chief named Scar-on-Face. I wouldn't be too welcome among my former captors."

"Bullshit!" another trooper blurted out.

Sgt. Mills' hard fist snapped out and struck Lone Wolf in the gut, a fraction of an inch below his solar plexus. The white warrior doubled over, gasping painfully. Gradually he straightened and spoke through panted breaths.

"Pay close attention, Sergeant Mills, all of you. I'll tell you again. I was a captive of the *Absaroka* for ten years. They admired my fighting skill for some reason, even made me a member of the Strong Heart warrior society. But I was always watched, never fully trusted. Then, when a chance came during a raid on the Sioux, I killed Scar-on-Face and escaped. After ten years, I've come to like the comfort of Indian clothing. Hell, two of your men are wearing moccasins, sergeant. Think about that."

Silence held for a long moment. Mills took a chewed stub of cigar and worried it into the corner of his mouth with thick, pouting lips. He struck a Lucifer match and held the flames to the blackened tip. He put the sulphur match out against the skin of Lone Wolf's right forearm.

"If we can't get the truth out of you here and now, we surely will when we take you in front of the colonel tomorrow."

At a nod from Mills, the beating began.

Lone Wolf ached from the crown of his head to the tip of his toes. His vision swam and his dry mouth tasted of caked blood. They had not hit him too hard, only often. Nothing seemed to be broken, though his ribs throbbed dully with an old and lasting pain. The sun had dropped below the mountains and only a wide band of deep crimson lined the western horizon. He'd never make it to Denver that day, his teetering mind told him in confusion.

When stupid men, with a set idea, listen to the truth over and over, he considered as his disorientation lessened, it does no good for the teller. Perhaps he should not have answered so readily. Let them pound bits of his story from him, one at a time. Then, maybe they would have believed him. Too late for that, his returning reason prompted. Only one thing mattered now. Somehow he had to devise an escape. Suddenly his stomach lurched and growled loudly at the heavenly aroma of meat roasting over a small campfire. Another problem to handle.

Would they feed him? He doubted it. Carefully he began to test his bonds.

He had nearly lost all circulation in his feet, tightly tied together, with further turns of rope at knees and thigh. The strand around his chest had been secured thoroughly, though his hands seemed somewhat loose in the restraints. Of course.

He had been struggling, resisting their efforts when tied. Now, relaxed, his hands no longer filled the loop of piggin' string. It offered a chance, though a slim one. Slowly, deliberately, he began to work his wrists, bending them so that his fingers reached the constraining bands.

A figure approached through the gathering dusk. Sergeant Archie Mills. "I brought you some grub. Not anything fancy. Rabbit an' some beans. I'll cut your hands loose to eat, then tie you up again."

"You are too kind," Lone Wolf told him sarcastically.

All the while his mind screamed at him. Tied! Again . . . could he manage to deceive them about the tightness again? He must. His only hope for escape depended on it.

NINE

A fine linen spread and napkins, silver rings, cut crystal candle holders, all on a highly polished rosewood table. Rebecca admired the lovely items, so alien in this low, roughly-made shanty. The meal had so far also been excellent.

"I managed to salvage a few things," Matt Peterson had explained to her, "before . . . before Tulley took over my father's house."

"What about your mother?"

"She's been dead now . . . for eight years. Anyway, I took what I could get. One thing that devil hasn't tried to do yet is grab the bank account. So I can eat well. Have you met our banker, Mr. Ross? He's as opposed to Tulley as the rest of us."

"No. I've not been inside town as yet."

"He's supposed to stop by for a few minutes tonight. He and Tom Allison. There's a lot the blacksmith can do for us."

"Yes. Like produce some kind of weapons."

"You heard about the edict Tulley put up today?"

"I saw one of the posters. Everyone is to surrender their firearms for the 'safety of the community.' Only Jake Tulley and his outlaws will be armed after that."

"No one will go along with it."

"I'm not so sure, Matt. There are always a few toadies, the craven who don't care about the loss of their rights. They will step forward first. After that

Tulley will have an excuse to conduct a search if the other people don't comply. The first thing a tyrant or a criminal wants to do is disarm the populace so they are helpless."

"That's mighty philosophical," Matt observed. "I wouldn't think that . . . being . . ."

"You mean after five years in an Oglala camp I shouldn't be that aware of the white man's ways?" Rebecca completed. "I was fourteen when we were . . . traded off. Before that my mother taught me well. It's only common sense and historically provable. Why did the Virginia Colony finally join the others against the Crown? One of the biggest factors was when the Royal Governor, Lord Dunsmore, foolishly sent Marines to seize the powder magazine and arsenal at Williamsburg. The people had heard King George called a tyrant by many orators. But when an officer of the Crown actually tried to take their guns, they knew he was."

"Can we solve our problem here without guns?" Matt asked hopefully.

"I'd like to think so. Tulley is a murderer and thief and the man who gives him orders has political ambitions. That makes a dangerous combination. Someone, either the U.S. marshal or the people of Grub Stake, is going to have to fight them. That means killing. What needs to be done is for everyone to resist the order, or to bury their weapons until needed." Rebecca paused, placed one hand lightly on Matt's. "How long did you say these men would be here? I had hoped we might . . ." She let it hang, teasing him.

Matt felt a stirring in his loins. Never had he encountered a woman who gave herself so fully to the enjoyment of love. His swelling organ still felt a pleasant warm tingling from the energetic activities of the previous night. He could hardly wait until they would be safely alone. Footsteps sounded outside the shanty.

"Matt, you there? This is Brian Ross."

"Come in, Mr. Ross. I . . . have the woman here I mentioned to you."

"Ah, the lady who faced down Tulley's killers the other day," Ross began as he entered. "A pleasure, Ma'am."

He extended a firm, well-manicured hand, which Rebecca took in her own tight grasp. "Glad to meet you, Mr. Ross. Matt says you are the banker here."

"That's right. At least while I can keep Tulley from taking over altogether." Ross made a sour face. "Which I fear won't be much longer. You and a, ah, friend have offered to help?"

"We will do what we can. Lone Wolf, ah, Brett Baylor, is on his way to Denver for help from the marshal. Meanwhile, I want to learn whom we can trust and what sort of weapons are available to fight Tulley's gang. Also their routine and average daily strength."

Ross snorted his amusement. "A regular little general, aren't you, Miss?"

"Rebecca Caldwell," Matt offered the belated introduction.

"I spent five years as a captive to the Sioux, Mr. Ross. You learn there how to fight in order to survive," she told the banker, a slight coolness to her voice. "I have searched for Tulley and fought him for nearly two months. Not long ago, Lone Wolf and I nearly destroyed his entire gang in a buffalo stampede. Jake Tulley is a tough opponent, but he can be beaten."

"Well, ah, Miss, uh, Caldwell, I didn't mean to disparage."

92

Of course you didn't, Rebecca thought in a flare of pique. Just to remind me that I'm only a slip of a girl and put me back in my proper place. "I understand, Mr. Ross," only too well, she concluded in her mind.

"Ah . . . Tom should be along in a moment."

"Fine," Rebecca said decisively to the banker. "We'll hold our discussion until then. A glass of wine, Mr. Ross?"

"Yes, that would be good, thanks. Where is your family, Miss Caldwell?"

"All dead, except for that low snake uncle of mine, Ezekial Caldwell. He's running the Mother Lode for Tulley."

Ross's eyebrows rose. "Oh? How did that come about?"

"It's a long story," Rebecca evaded. She handed Ross a glass of wine. "One I'd rather not go into right now. Mike Hoxsey or Kathlene O'Day can tell you about it, if it matters."

"Anything about a lovely woman matters to me," Ross returned gallantly.

"You flatter me, Mr. Ross."

"Not at all. And call me Brian."

"Thank you, Mr. Ross, but . . . after my experience, I'm sure you understand if I rely upon minor formality to . . . er, relearn white ways. No offense, you understand."

Ross nodded. A scrabbling knock sounded against the door post. Matt rose and opened up to reveal the huge-shouldered bulk of Tom Allison. "Come in, Tom."

After a brief exchange of pleasantries, Rebecca recounted what information she wanted and urged the three men to encourage everyone to resist the edict by hiding their arms. Then she concluded.

"I will be back in touch with you in two days. By

then I should have heard from Lone Wolf. We can finalize our plans at that time."

Ross had been impressed and his opinion revised. He assured her of his cooperation and departed with Tom Allison. After Matt closed the door behind them, he turned to his lovely guest.

"And now . . ."

"Yes, now . . ." Rebecca breathed huskily as she rose from the table.

Matt took her in his arms. Rebecca pressed herself tightly against him and felt the instant stir of life in his groin. They kissed longingly, tongues flirting, exploring, promising. Matt slid one hand to her narrow waist. Rebecca's pulse stampeded and her fingers traced the curlicues of Matt's right ear.

When the kiss ended, Rebecca gasped out her words. "These clothes. I've got to . . ."

"We've both got to get out of them," Matt amended.

They giggled like schoolyard conspirators.

"Let me," Rebecca urged and began to disrobe the handsome young man before her.

After his coat and vest, she pulled his shirt free and unbuttoned it. Matt breathed heavily and she could see his heart laboring under the smooth flesh of his hairless chest. Her fingers danced nimbly over his nipples, bringing instant erectness. A surge of sympathetic response swelled his elongated penis, which pressed insistently against her lower parts. She sighed with contentment and reached for his belt.

The buckle undone and buttons released, she pulled Matt's trousers down around his ankles and held the legs while he stepped out of them. His massive organ made a mountain peak in the front of his underdrawers.

"Aaaah," Matt sighed happily when Rebecca slid

one hand inside to encircle his pulsating manhood. "Suck me, Becky, do it like you did last night," he pleaded.

"Later," she murmured. She searched her memories for some new way to please him. She recalled the manner in which she had given surprising delight to her second Oglala husband and decided it would be perfect for tonight. She stepped away from Matt and quickly shed her clothing.

Candlelight made her golden skin even more lovely. She stood naked and trembling before Matt, a glow of passion in her deep blue eyes. Slowly, seductively, she walked to him. Her hands found the elastic sewn top of his underwear and pulled them away, revealing the full glory of his throbbing shaft. It swayed and ached to find release with this most beautiful, half-wild being who taunted him.

Rebecca spread her legs wide, clasped Matt's huge cock in both hands and rose on tiptoe. Her moisture flowed like a tiny creek, triggered by her own maddening desire. For a long, slow minute, she rubbed the sensitive tip of the gigantic cock in her wet cleft, lubricating it for its eventual plunge. Matt writhed and moaned in delight.

"Now . . . let's share our pleasure now," Becky urged him on. She rose a bit higher, positioned him and drove his greatness deep into her with a violent thrust of her hips.

"B-B-Becky!" Matt cried out in surprised delight. He felt her moist warmth enclosing him and he clutched her firm, round buttocks with both hands, impaling her further on the silken shaft. Of his own accord, he began to thrust his lance in and out, gaining momentum, delirious over this strange new way.

Rebecca held her own, matching him stroke for

stroke until she felt herself peaking. She brought her feet up off the floor and wrapped her legs around his churning waist, her head back, thrashing from side to side, in harmonious transport. Matt grunted softly and drove his massive prod deeper and faster until she cried out.

Now he slowed, paced himself while she slid down the far side of the incline and recouped to start up the next slope. Rebecca leaned back from him, supported by her arms, breasts swaying. Matt took one into his mouth, sucking urgently, tongue teasing the erect nipple.

"So good, Matt. Oh, so very good!" Rebecca cried out, her muscles tightening and slacking to give the most for the joy she received. "If only . . . this . . . would . . . never . . . never end!"

She gave a mighty heave that drove his hugeness to her secret depths and she felt the blunt tip slide against the open mouth of her throbbing womb.

"More!" she begged. "Deeper!"

In a rush, he penetrated where no man had gone before and they both felt the mighty rush toward paradise. The next instant they came together, a showering, shattering moment of emotional peak and sheer, magnificent physical contact and release.

How could friction, mere friction of internal parts, be so stupendous? Rebecca wondered before the blaze of lights engulfed her and she heard Matt grunting out spurt after spurt of his syrupy nectar.

"Oh . . . Oh, God . . . nobody . . . nothing has ever been so good, dearest Matt," Rebecca cooed to him while he staggered on weakened legs to the bed. He gently placed her on the backturned sheets, their bodies still connected by half his incredible, rigid length. Then he knelt between her wide-spread legs and thrust home once more.

"Again, darling?" she moaned. "Oh . . . yes! Yes . . . let's . . . do . . . it . . . again!"

After two hours of continuous, nearly frantic love-making, the sated pair lay back for rest. Sweet smiles curled their lips. Matt had one of Rebecca's breasts in his hand and she lightly grasped his slack maleness. Neither of them had ever known a lover quite like the present. So close had their hearts grown that they didn't need words to express that thought.

"The Indians must be tremendous lovers," Matt said at last.

"Oh, yes. They are. I learned a lot in Iron Calf's camp. They aren't ashamed of making love like white people. It's all . . . very open. They even make jokes about it."

"I'm not ashamed . . . are you?"

"No, Matt darling. Not in the least. When . . . when was your first time?"

"When I was thirteen."

"Then you got a big head start. I was sixteen."

Matt could hardly believe it. "To think you learned so much more than I in so short a time! It's marvelous. *You're* marvelous. I . . . I think I'm falling in love with you."

"Are you sure you're not just falling in lust?" Rebecca teased.

Matt felt a rekindling of life in his loins. "There's that, too. Yes. I . . . lust for you. But somehow, you're special, Becky. Not like some juvenile tumble in the hay."

Rebecca discovered the steaming solidity of his renewed erection. "Ah! Ol' devil lust is rearing his one-eyed head."

"About time, too," Matt agreed, his excitement mounting.

Rebecca bent low over Matt's hard, flat belly, her

97

mouth opening wide. "Aaah! Yes. That's it," Matt encouraged.

A soft snore sounded from the location of the single guard Sgt. Mills had posted on the small camp. Good, Lone Wolf thought. He counted on this undisciplined rabble not to be able to maintain a proper watch. Now he had lots to do.

Archie Mills had loosened his hands and allowed him to eat the sparse portions of rabbit, its leg joint still red and raw, and scoop of beans. Then the Volunteer sergeant began to retie his hands.

"Aren't you going to let me sit down?"

"You might feel more like talkin' if you have to sleep standin' up," Mills answered sharply.

Lone Wolf had clenched his fists and expanded his wrists all he could. Mills seemed not to notice. With everyone in camp asleep, it was time to get started.

Bristly hemp bit at Lone Wolf's skin while he sawed his wrists, seeking to stretch the bonds. When he felt them give a little, he tried to reach them with his fingers.

No luck.

Once more he see-sawed the rope, his skin chafing until blood ran. The thick moisture lubricated his fetters. He ground his hands together harder. Once more the binding slipped. Lone Wolf bent fingers numb with disuse until he felt the round braid of the hemp line. He tugged at it to no avail.

A muscle cramp speared through his shoulders, and he relaxed his efforts, panting softly through an open mouth. Off toward the fire a man grunted in his sleep, rolled over and began to snore again.

Lone Wolf relaxed and began his efforts once more. He forced himself backward by pressure on his aching legs, then wrenched his wrists back and forth, feeling a tempting looseness. Freedom seemed so close. More blood poured over the dry hemp and suddenly it gave again.

This time, three fingers closed over a strand and he inched his bindings toward his knuckles. Slowly the turns of rope came. So achingly slowly. The cramp spiked him again and he had to stop, easing the strain from his bunched muscles.

Refreshed, he started again.

Release took him by surprise. One moment he was still bound, the next a soft plop sounded when the piggin' string hit the ground and his arms swung free. He brought his arms around in front of him and massaged the wrists. Still no sound from the Colorado Volunteer soldiers. Lone Wolf's left hand found the knot that held him bound around the chest.

Whoever had tied it knew his knots. Lone Wolf's fingers struggled impotently at the tight kink. Sweat glistened on his arms, despite the chill of night, and more drops slid down his forehead and stung his eyes. Still he labored silently.

Backward, his mind shouted at him. Do it backward of the way it was tied. His aching fingers closed around the right loop and he gave it a violent tug. Instantly the knot fell apart. Next he went for the line that bound his thighs.

He could use both hands on this one, he discovered. Good. It should go quickly that way. A twist and pull and it did. Lone Wolf let it fall away.

Now he bent forward, seeking the final restraint at his knees. He searched without success. The knot had been tied in the back. Fiery pain shot through his calves when he forced his legs back against the rough bark of the pine. Overhead an owl hooted mournfully. Wind soughed through the needles. One of the irregulars coughed wetly, hawked out a wad of phlegm and settled back in his blankets. Lone Wolf stood motionless for two long minutes, then began again.

The pain remained, insistent, debilitating. His fingers closed over the rope, sensing the hoped for slack, and he pulled with all his might. The scrape of hemp over bark sounded deafening loud in his ears. He paused after only a foot and waited.

No call of alarm from the sleeping men.

Again he pulled, feeling the burn of the braid over his kneecaps. He gained another foot. His right hand could feel the knot. Another hard tug. There! He had it.

In three seconds, Lone Wolf undid the knot and let himself gratefully to the ground. He freed his feet and bit back a groan of agony when blood rushed back into the constricted vessels below his ankles. When he tried to stand, he tottered drunkenly and had to catch himself against the tree. Every second spelled mortal danger to him. Cautiously he extended one foot in front of the other. He gingerly placed his weight on it. Flares of agony raced up his leg, but he forced another step. And another. He got his bearings and started unerringly toward the small picket line. He placed his hands to his lips.

The nightbird call that Lone Wolf uttered cautioned his horse to remain quiet. He neared the rope picket, soothing the other animals in a soft whisper. Quickly he located his saddle and weapons, slung them on the Indian pony's back and released the rein from its tie.

Lone Wolf led his mount for a mile away from the Volunteers' camp before he cinched down the saddle and swung astride. Yes, he thought ruefully. Rebecca had been right. He'd put all the miles he could between him and his enemy, along the road to Denver, then, at first light, he would stop long enough to shave off his roach and change into the pair of woolen trousers and flannel shirt in his saddle bags. Like it or not, from now on, on this mission, he would be a white man.

TEN

Perhaps it had been love's blindness, Rebecca thought later on, that had made her incautious. She had been summoned to Allison's smithy for a report on what weapons were available and what the blacksmith could produce — pike heads from axes, long, slender spear blades, billhooks — and had left the rear way, her mind on Matt Peterson and the wonderful prospect of their love making in the evening to come. She had rounded a corner . . .

. . . And ran into three of Tulley's gunhawks.

"We-e-ll, lookie here," Long Tom Wheeler drawled. "This is a new one, by Glory. What say we have us a little sample?" He groped the stained crotch of his denim trousers with a thicky horny hand, deeply ridged with callus and rope burns.

"Naw, that'd only get the boss mad at us."

"Hell, Murf, we ain't even in town an' I'm itchin to dip my wick."

"If you can't control that over-sized sausage of yours, Long Tom, maybe you otta go to the outhouse and whup him a good one," Murf snapped. "Remember what the boss said. We're not to touch any of the locals. This is gonna be our town an' we do things right."

"She ain't no local gal. Look at that squaw dress she's wearin'." Wheeler stopped suddenly and one hand strayed to his face, dirty fingernails scratching at a cluster of smallpox scars on his cheek. "Say, what was that about some gal all tricked out in Injun clothes huntin' for Tulley's scalp?"

Murf peered closely at Rebecca. The other outlaw did also. All three exchanged an avaricious glance. Tulley had put a price on the girl's head, a thousand in gold now, and if this turned out to be the one. . .

"Let's take her to Zeke," Long Tom suggested. "He'll know the truth of it."

For this risky trip into town, Rebecca had concealed her .38 Smith & Wesson in her beaded purse. At sight of the three hardcases, she had stuck her hand into the drawstring opening. When the trio moved toward her, she hastily drew and shot the silent one in the chest. He uttered a soft sigh and fell in a heap, silent in death as he had been in life.

Then the other two leaped on her, wrestling the gun away.

"We brought you something, Zeke," Long Tom Wheeler announced when he and Murf dragged Rebecca into Ezekial Caldwell's office.

Ezekial looked up from his desk, eyes widening and brows arching toward his receding hairline. "Wha . . . Hummm. One of Flora Belle's chippies try to escape?"

"That we don't know. But we was wonderin', considerin' the clothes she is wearing an' all . . ." Wheeler let it hang.

Ezekial pretended a close scrutiny, though he had instantly recognized his niece. "You mean about the, ah, woman who is after Jake? Hummm. No. I don't think so. Let's see her face. She was close enough to put a bullet in this shoulder, so I ought to recognize her."

Wheeler complied, raising Rebecca's resisting head

by a yank on her hair. Ezekial leaned close, his eyes glittering with malevolence. "No. Not the one. But a loose woman, all the same. No respectable white woman would dress like that. Now she's here, we might as well take advantage. You fellers can go. Flora Belle can handle this from here on."

Reluctantly, Wheeler and Murf shuffled out of the office. At the door, Wheeler turned back. "We caught her, right, Zeke?" At Caldwell's nod, he went on. "Then I figger I got a foot of pecker that has first call on her services when Flora Belle turns her out. Is that right?"

A wicked smile lifted the corners of Ezekial's mouth.

"That sounds like an excellent idea. Why not? To the victor goes the spoils and all that, eh? You can count on it, Wheeler. And for now, drinks on the house for both of you."

After the two gunslingers had departed to enjoy their reward, Ezekial turned back to Rebecca. "And now, my sweet little niece. I have some great plans for you. Oh, yes. A more fitting end, I could not conceive."

Still dazed from her roughing up and frog-march delivery to her uncle's office, Rebecca looked at him with blazing eyes, trying to sort out the meaning of all she had heard. Ezekial saw her confusion and took pleasure in clarifying the issue for her.

"Oh, yes. A Sioux whore wouldn't be familiar with what we discussed a moment ago. Flora Belle Chase is a madam. She is in charge of the bawdy house I'm running here in the Mother Lode. She's going to 'turn you out.' In other words, dear Rebecca, she's going to make you into a prostitute."

"No! I . . . I'll never go along with that. Never."

Ezekial laughed, a wicked sound that seemed to swell and fill the room. "You won't have any choice in the matter. When Flora Belle gets through with you, you'll beg for men to stick their dingledangles deep inside you. It'll be a lot like the Oglala camp, I imagine. Just desserts I would say."

"Nothing like that happened," Rebecca snapped back, her own anger rising. "I was untouched . . . until I . . . I married. I had a child."

"Oh? Well then, that makes me a grand-uncle," Ezekial chortled, enjoying this shaming of his dangerous niece.

"No. He was killed in a Crow raid."

"A boy, eh? Just as well. One less filthy savage in the world."

"You bastard!" Despite her anger and fiery resolve, tears of grief and frustration spilled from Rebecca's eyes.

Ezekial's hard hand lashed out and slapped her soundly on one cheek. "Dinkum! Hey, Dinkum!" he bellowed.

A moment later a twisted little man with filthy face and grimy hands, the saloon swamper, appeared in the doorway. "Yes, sir, Mr. Caldwell?"

"Tell Flora Belle I want to see her. I've got a new inmate for her."

"No!" Rebecca shouted. "Never, you filthy pig!" She leaped at her uncle while Dinkum turned to obey his orders. Ezekial struck her with a balled fist in the ribs under her left armpit. It sent her sprawling into a chair. Pain exploded and Rebecca subsided with a stifled whimper.

"Oh, this is going to be delicious revenge," Ezekial raved, walking about his office, touching a crystal decanter of brandy on a sideboard, adjusting a portrait of Jeff Davis that hung on one wall. "Tulley need never know. I'll have you all to myself. Flora Belle will break that stubborn will of yours. In no time at all, she'll tame you, then we'll shame you to the point of begging for death. Oh, and sometimes, I will come and watch. It should be entertaining, educatin', too. When I tire of the game, I might . . . yes, I might even let Bobby O'Toole have you."

A shaft of pure fear burned away the anger in Rebecca's breast. She had seen the depredations O'Toole called sexual pleasure. Her stomach roiled with nausea. To be given to Bobby O'Toole!

"Oh, you poor dear," a cawing voice that attempted to sound solicitous spoke close by Rebecca's head. "What have they done to you? Leavin' you here like this in a dark room. It's terrible, that's what it is."

A shaft of bright light stabbed at Rebecca's eyes when the black-painted blind rose suddenly. She put a hand over her face to reduce the painful intensity. Then she felt a pressure on the side of the mattress on which she lay.

"I'll bet they ain't fed you, either. Here, take this. It will help you keep food down when I bring it later."

"What . . . what is it?" Rebecca asked dreamily, her tongue testing the sticky, biting sweetness.

"It's a sugar ball, dearie. Suck on it or swallow it down. It's so you can build your strength back. An' don't worry. I'll be back soon. Real soon."

"Oh, please. Tell me. Where am I? What's going on?" Rebecca implored in a weary, little-girl voice.

"Time for that later. You've been sick. I'm here to care for you. Trust me."

Out in the hallway, Ezekial Caldwell spoke quietly to the woman. "How is it going, Flora Belle?"

"Fine. I've only had her for a day and already she's doped to the gills. Only a little longer and then I'll break her in."

Ezekial smiled coldly. "Like old times, Flora. Always got to sample the goods first, eh?"

"Why not? That way the girl gets a little pure love before going into the trade." She patted a stray puff of her frizzy red-blonde hair, disciplined it into place and raised her chin defiantly toward Ezekial.

Flora Belle resented any reference, particularly by men, to her preference for young girls. It had been a part of her life for as long as she could remember. Well, at least since the age of eleven, when . . . when she had taken piano lessons from Helen. A vivacious young woman, Helen had quickly charmed parents in St. Louis and acquired a large clientele of hopeful piano students. From the first time she had rewarded Flora Belle Chase for excellent performance with a hug and a kiss, and had it returned with warmth and fervor, she began to teach Flora Belle a great deal more than four finger exercises in the key of G. She had been a quick and eager learner, Flora Belle recalled.

"We're two of a kind," Helen had whispered to her one afternoon as they lay naked in Helen's big bed, exhausted by the urgency of their lovemaking. By this time their affair had gone on for two years. Flora Belle had blossomed into womanhood and her preference set. There had been others since Helen, many others. To hell with it, Flora Belle shook off her reflective mood, I am what I am . . . and I love it.

"I figure she'll be ready for a man by some time tomorrow."

"Good. Make it in the blue room, so I can watch through that hole in the painting."

"You're a dirty old man, Ezekial."

"I have my reasons. Never mind. She's someone's white squaw and I'm curious about the gyrations them heathen red niggers get their women up to. That's all."

"Oh, of course, Ezekial. Of course."

How soft and fuzzy the world is. The black-haired, naked girl on the bed languidly blinked her dark blue eyes and wiggled her body against the sheets, enjoying the sensuous feel. She no longer knew who she was, didn't care. Or where, or when. Only one thing filled her consciousness. She longed for the gentle woman with the coarse voice and wonderful sweet sugar pills to return soon. She wanted this marvelous, drifting feeling to go on and on forever. A dim part of her mind told her she could do so only as long as she had the pills. Vaguely she sensed the door opening.

Flora Belle Chase stood in the opening, a happy smile on her face. She watched the girl loll her head toward her, a beatific smile of anticipation on the lovely full lips.

"Did . . . you . . . Did you bring . . . it?" the captive inquired in a foggy voice.

"Yes. Of course I did, hon. Only . . . this time we wait a little. Are you all right?"

"I . . . feel fine. Won-der-fulll." The opium-drugged girl blinked. Was this another of her happy dreams? It looked like the woman who brought her the marvelous pills was taking off her clothes.

Then she felt a pressure when the naked woman climbed into bed with her. Fingers probed for her cleft, spreading the lips in a familiar and exciting way. No! something inside her warned. This was not right. It should . . . should be a . . . a man. She tried to pull away.

"Now, now. Come to me dearie. Be nice to Flora Belle and she'll be nice to you. Relax. Spread those lovely legs and let me find your pleasure nest. That's it . . . that's . . . Ow!"

"Get away from me!" For a moment, revulsion had conquered the euphoria of the drug. "Get away or I'll hit you again."

"No you won't, Missy. You're mine now. All mine. You do what you're told or you don't get your nice little sugar pill. Now spread your legs and let me at that muff."

"You're sick! I . . . uh . . ." slowly the cloud cover of the drug seeped over the fire of rebellion. "I'll . . ."

A rough hand spread into the sparsely thatched triangle at the juncture of her legs, insistent fingers probing deeper. "Spread it!" a harsh, cawing voice commanded. "Come on, bitch. Let Flora Belle at that tasty bush."

Again ancient mores rose to give clarity to the bewildered girl. She struck out with a closed fist this time, raising a red spot under Flora Belle's left eye, that rapidly swelled.

"You cunt! Filthy slut! Goddamn you, you'll pay for that," Flora Belle raged. Quickly she dressed and stalked out of the room. Behind her the frightened, confused and revolted girl burst into tears.

She came back ten minutes later. In her hands she held a pair of manacles, a coil of rope and a long whip. She put the cuffs on the feebly struggling girl, attached the rope, which she fed through a pulley in the ceiling. With grunting effort, she hauled the girl upright. Then she began to ply the lash, gauging her strokes to provide great pain, but not to cut the precious commodity of that golden flesh. Oh, God, how she had wanted this one. The most beautiful body she had ever seen. Five . . . six . . . seven . . . the whipping went on.

Finally satisfied, Flora Belle ceased the flogging. She produced a jar of salve and began to administer it to the weals on the girl's back. She alternated swatches of the cooling, healing balm with hot, trembling kisses, missing no part of the unconscious victim's body.

"There, there, my little one. It's all over now. If you be a good girl it will never happen again. Oh, you are so lovely. So very pretty. I must . . . I simply must kiss you and make you well. Then, later, you can have another sugar pill. Two. It will let you sleep and feel all better tomorrow. Oh, oh . . ."

"I will not!" Rebecca yelled into Flora Belle's face. In order to perform with a male customer, the girls had to be dried out of their drug stupor. Although still hazy, Rebecca had her wits about her enough to refuse the demand that she work as a soiled dove. For her defiance, she received a slap on both cheeks.

"You will do it, or more of the whip, you foolish little bitch. You're here and here you are going to stay. So why not lie back and enjoy it. How long has it been since you ate?"

"Why, uh . . . ah . . . yester . . ."

"Three days, bitch. And it will be another three if you don't cooperate. Now, you're gonna spread your legs for every man-jack who wants you. That's the way of your life, it always was and always will be. Get used to the idea. And . . . you'll not get any more sugar pills unless you do." A knowing gleam illuminated Flora Belle's eyes.

"Oh . . . I . . ." A sudden craving, that sent her stomach into a queasy swirl of nausea, swept over the helpless girl. "Oh, I . . . I've got to have them. Please, don't take them away. It's all that makes life . . . good."

"Then get down there in that bed of yours and wait for a customer. You fuck like a mink or you get no pill."

Tears squeezed from under tightly clenched lids. "Oh, please. Please . . ."

Ten minutes later, the miserable girl, who no longer knew her name or history, heard hard boot-heels scrape on the floor, smelt the odor of tobacco and whiskey. A raspy voice murmured above her over the sound of clothes hitting the floor.

"My, yer right purty, honey. I'm sure gonna get my money's worth on this one. Man, oh, man."

The girl felt his hard, rough organ enter her dry passage and the pain brought a moment's clarity. Inside her, while he grunted and strained, something died a little.

ELEVEN

"You can't believe it, Jake," Roger Styles enthused, his face alight with enthusiasm. "The whole town is floating with boatloads of money. Most of it in nice untraceable gold. Everyone wants to make deals. Every property owner, businessman and grifter wants his special interest to receive priority and preferential treatment when the new legislature is formed and Colorado becomes a state."

"Sounds nice . . . for you," Jake Tulley growled.

"For you, too," Roger replied quickly. "That's why I suggested we meet here, in Cripple Creek, where no one knows either of us. I've already made several deals, with enough profit to cover the operation in Grub Stake for the next two months and leave a tidy bonus for you and me. Here," he gestured toward a small trunk that sat in the corner of the rear room of the Cripple Creek assay office, which Roger had rented for their secret meeting. "That valise holds the gold. It's the agreed pay for your men, plus a small gratuity for each one. There's nothing like it in the world, Jake."

Bitter Creek Jake relaxed. He let a satisfied smile spread on his face. Roger Styles could be a bastard at times, but he had always been generous with money. "So you're all set to become a lesi . . . legislator, eh?"

"I've met some powerful men, influential fellahs who are just like you an' me underneath. Get a little liquor in 'em and a dolly on their knee an' they're common as dirt. You know what they say, a stiff pecker has no conscience. Well, I figure to clinch the deal once you have Grub Stake toein' the line. We'll bring down a few, any who are being difficult, and let them have the run of your bawdy house there."

"What do you think would happen if they were to be caught *en flagrante?*" Roger's eyes twinkled with avarice.

"Ya mean with their pants down?"

"Exactly! They'll cooperate, because they'll have to. We can even have one of those Brady fellers, you know, the ones who take the daguerreotypes, on hand. They'll see to it I'm made a member of the 'Club,' or their wives will get copies of all the juicy evidence."

"I gotta hand it to you, Roger, you sure got the brains."

"Thank you, Jake. And you've got the muscle to back up our plans. Together we make an unbeatable team. Now here's what I have figured for Grub Stake." Roger paused a moment and poured three glasses of fine quality brandy. He handed one to Jake, another to Luke Wellington and sipped deeply of the third.

"First thing next week, you announce that there will be elections held on the first Tuesday of next month. Then present a slate of candidates, the only ones permitted to run, with me offered as state legislator, you as mayor, Luke," he motioned to the silent gunslinger who sat backward on an oak chair, arms folded over the back, chin on hands. "Luke to be the county sheriff. Pick whomever you want for the town counsel. But one thing, keep that disgusting swine, O'Toole, out of it."

"You can count on that. Though we do need someone to clean out the public outhouses." Tulley guffawed. "Maybe Commissioner of Sanitation? It'd suit. An' he could sniff all the toilet seats he wanted."

"Jesus! It must be infectious. You're getting as rank as O'Toole."

"Just jokin', Roger," Tulley came back, sobered. "This is good brandy."

"My personal label. Something new since Denver. Now, the elections will go the way we want them, because we'll be the only ones running."

"What if people insist on nominating someone else? Or write in a candidate?" Luke Wellington queried.

"Who'll be counting the ballots?" Roger asked scornfully.

"Oh, uh, yeah." A grin spread. "Now I see."

"So, that makes everything legal. Then, with a little friendly persuasion, there should be no trouble getting me into the inner circle of the new state government. Who knows? Maybe in a few years I'll be governor of Colorado."

"I'll settle for being the mayor of the biggest whorehouse and gamblin' town in the country," Jake advised. "That's enough politics for me."

"It's yours as long as you like Jake. You mentioned earlier about some resistance from people in Grub Stake?"

"Yeah. Yeah, a smart-ass miner named Mike Hoxsey is stirrin' up trouble. He ran my boys off his place twice with fused sticks of dynamite. He an' the feller who figured to be mayor, Bart Carstairs, they're the ring leaders."

"How many people do they represent?"

"Maybe half a dozen. Couldn't be many more. I'd have to include that punk son of the saloon owner, Peterson. He got all sour when I throwed him outta that fancy house. But I don't think he can even handle a gun."

"That doesn't matter. We cannot afford dissension. Any opposition is too much opposition. You've disarmed everyone?"

"The posters have gone up. So far, uh . . . we ain't got any guns turned in. I'll have the boys shake up the place a little. After all, the law's the law, right?"

"Now you're thinkin' the right way. Have you heard anything about, uh, Rebecca Caldwell?"

"That bitch! Only that she's supposed to be ridin' our backtrail. I got boys posted on the lookout for her. If she shows around Grub Stake, she'll never leave there alive."

"Sounds good. Then the final thing is that you are to put pressure on these malcontents. I want this Hoxsey eliminated. At once."

"This is really the big time, huh, Long Tom?" Clyde Morton asked the sullen gunslinger. "Gettin' orders by telegraph. Whooie! Am I glad I signed on with a class outfit like this."

"Shut your jaw and pay attention. We're gettin' close to that mine."

"Boy is Hard Rock ever gonna get a surprise."

"Last time, as I hear it, you left his place with yer tail betwixt yer legs, scared of a little stick of dynamite."

"Lay off me, huh, Long Tom?" Clyde complained, stung by the memory of his humiliation.

"We'll pull off here and wait. We left town ahead of him, so he should be along any minute."

"We gonna just off and plug him?"

"What else? Do you want him to have time to light up another stick of dynamite?"

* * *

Hard Rock Mike weaved a little in the saddle. He'd had a few drinks at the Mother Lode, keepin' an eye on the enemy, of course. Not enough to be a skinful, mind, but they sure hit his head at the altitude, with the hot sun burning down. He leaned forward and patted the sturdy neck of his trustworthy mule.

"Jennifer, yer my treasure," he reassured the animal. "Where'd I be without you?"

Jennifer rolled a dubious eye.

"Yep. For one thing I would be stumblin' along this trail on foot, wishin' for another drink. Fact of the matter, I sure could use one anyhow." Mike fished out his canteen and took a long swallow. "Aaagh! Luke-warm an' not even bad whiskey, just pure, awful ol' water."

He rummaged in his pockets, at last locating an oval half-pint bottle with the profile of George Washington molded into the glass. "Hummm. Howdy, George. Have a drink? Don't mind iffin I do, thankee."

The bottle neck disappeared into a dark hole in Mike's facial hair. His prominent Adam's apple worked violently for three long swigs before he pulled the container from his mouth. Mike looked closer onto fifty than his thirty-eight years. Times had been hard, no matter what he said to make little of his difficulties. For a while, after he had lost his wife and daughter, he didn't care if he made it or not. Those who knew him didn't believe he would. He'd taken to the bottle. Hard, two-fisted, shit-in-your-pants, falling down drunk boozing bouts that left him completely blank on what had happened.

Then his sons found him passed out, face down in a rain-filled gutter one winter's night. Pneumonia nearly finished what the liquor had begun. When he at last came out of it, he decided on the trip west to get away from all the bad memories. Since then, though his station in life had hardly improved, his outlook had. Beyond an occasional beer, he rarely drank, tied one on no more than once a year. Today, though, the whiskey seemed to provide a safety valve, to release much of the pressure of the present problem.

Mike could brawl with the best of them, this he knew. He need fear no man, with gun, knife or fist. Yet, Jake Tulley and twenty-some men presented a much more formidable enemy than he could safely confront alone. He didn't think their chances, all together, were that good. Even with that feisty li'l Caldwell girl.

Though rumors traveled fast and he had heard about the blazing confrontation between Rebecca Caldwell and the Tulley gang, word had it she'd chased them right out of the Black Hills country and left an impressive number of dead owlhoots in her wake. That kind of spirit might turn the tide for them. He put away the whiskey bottle and drubbed his knees into his mule's ribs.

"Come on, Jennifer. It's gettin' on to noonin' an' we got boilt beans an' fatbacks waitin' us."

He started to add, "When I get around to cookin' 'em," when the first bullet smashed into him, low on the right side.

Hard Rock Mike somersaulted off his mule, heels over head. Three slugs went astray in the process. A fourth gouged meat from his ribcage and a large wet stain spread on his flannel shirt. Another drilled a neat hole through his left breast pocket.

"That's enough," Long Tom Wheeler commanded. "He's dead. Let's head back to town. I'm hungry."

TWELVE

Hands. Groping, probing, punishing hands. Would they never go away? Everything seemed so hazy and indistinct. Only the hands had substance, touching her, stroking, pinching, always and forever. Where was this place? What was she doing there? The sole release from the touch and smell of tobacco, whiskey and male lust came from the marvelous sugar pills. The woman brought them. Brown, sticky and chewy. Escape from the seemingly endless procession of hands and bodies pressed hard against her own. With the pills came the floating and dreaming, pleasant blackness, opening at last into . . .

. . . Bright, clear blue sky ranged above in a spherical vault, broken here and there by delicate white puffs of cloud. All around she heard the drumming of hoofs. Horses neighed and from the flanks came the sharp, joyful cries of the warriors riding guard. Children shrilled and ran in among the moving band, oblivious of danger, playing kick ball and "hide-the-bone." The women and old people trouped along in the vanguard. Far ahead, more warriors led the procession, among them her beloved husband, Four Horns. How wonderful it was to be free! No longer a slave, subjected to harsh voices of criticism. Now she had friends and a man who loved her. A lodge of her own. A place in the Oglala band. And soon, there would be three of them. She hoped it would be a son to please Four Horns. Presently they would be back in their own lands, camped by the sandy-bottomed stream that meandered across the prairie south of the Black Hills. Now, though, the village of Iron Calf moved rapidly. There had been a raid on the hated *Pani*.

She shuddered when she remembered that raid. It had been in revenge for a horse stealing venture by the Pawnee. Needlessly some Oglala herd boys had been murdered. Iron Calf called for total revenge. Scouts had trailed the stolen horses, located the offending camp of *Pani*. Then the entire village set out. She had stood with the other women and children on a ridge overlooking the Pawnee village. The Oglala warriors had slipped down through the grass, wriggling on their bellies, silent and deadly. Others waited on horseback to strike the village. When the signal came, the infiltrator rose up and made off with the entire horse herd. Angry warriors of the enemy camp charged toward them. Then the slaughter began.

Arrows hummed through the still, early morning air, war clubs flashed, their stone heads slick and red. Dust boiled up and the center of the conflict disappeared in a howling mob of fighting men. From here and there tiny puffs of smoke appeared, followed by the thump of the reports. The rattle of gunfire increased. The Pawnee had firearms, too. Flames began to appear and smoke billowed from several lodges. The hide tents roared and crackled. Screams of the wounded and dying filled the air. A swarm of mounted warriors wheeled and charged across the embattled village. A small boy broke out of the confusion and ran on chubby legs, balled fists to his eyes, his thin wail of terror sounding clearly over the melee.

119

Then a warrior charged down on him, scooped the child up and carried him toward the hill, a legitimate spoil of war. Some of the *Pani* managed to escape. They ran with powerful strides until clear of the valley of death where they caught up stray horses. They would ride swiftly to the nearest village of their people and enlist aid. Then Four Horns broke away from the dwindling battle and rode toward her, his face alight with pride, one arm aloft, a dripping scalp in his hand. Ah, Four Horns . . . Four Horns . . . strange, she knew his name, but not her own. Who was she? . . .

. . . "There you are, dearie. All awake now? That's fine. Did you enjoy your little tryst? Oh, he was a real stallion, wasn't he? Here, I have just what you want. A little candy. Sweet and spicy. Take it, take it. Enjoy while you can. There'll be another gentleman to see you soon. That's it." The cawing voice seemed familiar to her. She had heard it before.

She tried to focus on the figure that bent over the bed. A strange pink cloud seemed to surround the face. The eyes held no warmth, no compassion, though the words sounded kind enough. And, yes, oh, yes. The magical, wonderful, soothing medicine of the candy. Sugar pills, the woman called them. She reached out languidly and accepted the proffered relief. The darkness closed in even before she finished chewing.

Out in the hall, Ezekial Caldwell spoke to Flora Belle Chase when she came out of the room. "You're doing rather well. How long before she's tractable?"

"Another day, two at the most. She has a lovely body, that one. A shame to waste it on *men.*"

"Flora, Flora, my love, you amaze me. Take good

care of her, will you. I want to see her on the floor downstairs turning tricks like all the rest."

"Never fear. My method always works."

Ezekial turned away and went down the stairs to his office.

Thin slivers of light showed around the black-painted window blind. The world seemed to pulsate, drawing close in sharp focus, then racing away into fuzzy limbo. Her body ached. Oh, how she needed more of the medicine. Her ravaged system craved it and her mind screamed for release once again. Why hadn't the woman come as usual? A door opened, dimly perceived, and the woman in the red cloud came in. She carried a plate of food. The aroma made the girl's stomach lurch.

"Here's your breakfast, dearie. Eat it all, you have to keep up your strength."

"No. I . . . I feel sick. Please, give me one of the pills. I need it badly."

"Ah, so that's it, is it?" the voice feigned surprise. "Bless me, maybe you are right. Here, take it. That's a good girl. Chew it up now. Good. Keep chewing. And swallow now. Oh, very good."

Ah, so nice. So peaceful to drift off like this . . .

. . . He came to her in the night. Young and strong, smelling sweetly of sage. She had prepared a hidden nest, outside Iron Calf's village. It would be an adventure. An opportunity to be truly alone for the first time in a long while. She waited eagerly until he stepped into the low hut made of cut pine and cedar boughs. Wordlessly, he knelt at her side.

Her hands darted to the front of his loincloth. She

felt the heated bulge there and thrilled to the touch. Quickly she removed his clothing and threw back the buffalo robe that covered her nakedness. Four Horns' eyes widened in appreciation of her flawless body, swollen now with the child she carried. He reached out to gently caress the rising belly.

"You are so beautiful," he murmured. "But . . . is it . . . is it safe? Should we be doing this with the little one on the way?"

"Of course, my love." She grasped his swollen penis and began to stroke it marveling, as always at the size of it and its silky texture. It felt good wherever she put it. In her hand, her tingling cleft or deep in her mouth, each had its own pleasure for her. Idly she wondered if she had become a wanton. Surely it was never meant for a woman to enjoy lovemaking so much. In fact, she often wanted it more than Four Horns. Often? Always!

Yes, she always longed for the hot, iron-hard bulk of him to bring her joy beyond anything she had ever experienced. Oh, how lovely it was to have it surging inside her. And, when he sighed softly and exploded his syrup deep in her pulsating cavity, how very delicious it felt. She would never . . . never get enough. Deftly, sensing his rising passion, she increased the speed of her strokes. His hand went out, found the wet, burning center of her being and began to manipulate it with long, dexterous fingers. Little shivers of delight coursed through her body. When neither of them could endure it further, she lay back, legs wide-spread.

Slowly, Four Horns lowered himself over her. The swaying wand of his maleness bobbed before her entranced eyes and she watched it fixedly as it nestled tightly against the top of her swollen mound. She relaxed the small muscles there, widening herself in preparation for the magnificence of his entry. She trembled in anticipation, raising her hips to accommodate his hugeness. Then, with a shudder, he plunged home, driving his throbbing phallus deep inside, piercing the veils and plumbing the slick passage to her secret place. She moaned and called out for more. Four Horns hesitated, ignorant of the mechanics of womanhood and fearful for the child she carried.

"Oh, no, no. Keep it up, my beloved. More, more . . . all of it."

They surged and strained together until she felt her body as a separate entity and with a whirl surged over into completion. On they labored, bodies glistening with a thin sheen of sweat, striving for yet another peak to conquer. Four Horns breathed harshly and ground his hips in wide circles to heighten the pleasure for them both. Her legs crossed over his narrow waist and her own rhythm went wild with the approach of blissful oblivion.

Like mating creatures of the wild, they cried out in unison when the spectacular moment arrived. Then came the soft, sinking wonder of it all.

Through the haze of her delight, she knew the warming truth. He was hers, only hers, and so very good for her . . .

. . . Darkness surrounded her and her mouth tasted of ashes. The pill had done its work and worn off. She opened gummy eyes to a dimly lighted room. The door opened and the pink cloud woman entered. Immediately her craving for the miraculous sugar pills increased.

"A-another. I need another pill."

"No, dearie," the voice cawed at her. "Not now.

You have a gentleman to entertain."

"Oh, please. Please let me have one more. I promise to be good. Really."

"Afterward. Always after." She went away and, a moment later, the door opened again.

An indistinct form stood there, silhouetted in the light from the hall. Her hazy vision permitted no details, but she smelled sour sweat, tobacco and cheap liquor. The visitor advanced, rubbing his hands together in glee.

"My, my, ain't this a nice surprise. You're going to be real good for me, eh, sweetie. Oh, I can tell. Lordy what a body." The speaker began to remove his clothes. "C'mon, now. How do you like it? Me on top? You on top? Oh, I know now. Roll over there, little one. You like it from the back, like my lit'l pard. He ain't here, 'cause he's only a tyke. But I swear, next year, somehow I'm gonna see he gets a little poon. Make a man outtn' him. Then we can be real partners . . . an' no one needs to know what we do them cold nights in winter, snowed in up in the hills." A large object appeared in his hands and he stroked it fondly.

She felt pressure on the bed beside her and then the man forced himself into her. Pain radiated and she cried out, despite the repeated admonition from the pink cloud woman not to disturb the other customers. The man in bed with her grunted and pumped his hips. She felt nothing but pain . . . and shame and fear. Why was this happening? Desperately she tried to recapture the wondrous escape of the pills. If only she had one. It would dampen the misery, soothe the pain. All that counted in life were the pills.

"There now, all through? My he enjoyed himself, didn't he?"

"The pill. Can I have it now?"

"Later, dearie, you have to eat something first. It's breakfast time."

"But . . . I just had breakfast."

"No. That was ages ago. My how some people forget. Now eat up and we'll see about a pill then."

"But why can't I have it now?"

"What you need is some refreshment, and some tender loving care."

"I . . . yes. I so wonder . . ." the girl let it hang.

She tried to eat the food, but it rebelled in her stomach. She gagged and stumbled toward a chamber pot on the shelf under the washstand. She barely made it in time. Then the pink haired woman came to her, holding her shoulders and supporting the heavy crockery container while she heaved into it. "There, there, love. Poor baby is sick. Get it all out. Throw away the poison," she crooned to the naked girl. "There, Flora loves you. She'll care for you." Her hands began to caress the bare flesh, gently touching the pert breasts, rubbing the stomach, working lower.

Flora Belle's fingers found their goal and entered the tightened ridges of the sparsely tufted mound. Diligently she worked deeper. It brought a gasp from the girl. This . . . this was like nothing she had experienced so far. Flora Belle helped her to her feet and gave her water, all the while using one hand to manipulate the sensitive linings of her abused cleft.

"Come now, back to bed, dear one. What you need, perhaps, is a teensy bit of the sugar pill. Maybe half of one. Yes, Flora Belle will care for you, my honey." At the bedside, she opened a small metal tin taken from one pocket. She used a sharp fingernail to divide one opium ball and gave the girl the smaller portion.

Immediately after swallowing, she began to drift.

Only vaguely she sensed a presence close at hand. She saw, as though in slow motion, Flora Belle remove her dress and underthings. A slight pressure indicated the woman's entry in the bed. Then she was kissing and caressing the unresisting body of the girl. The jolt of sexual excitement brought instant clarity to her mind.

"What are you doing! That's . . . that's awful. Get out of here. Get out of my bed."

"No. I need you, I want you very much. It drove me mad to watch those men running their hands over your body. To see them getting their pleasure while you had none. This is the only way, the only way a woman can be fulfilled."

"No! You're terrible and it's filthy. Get out—get out—get out!"

A sudden iciness entered Flora Belle's voice. "We'll see about that, Miss Bitch. Yes and soon, too. You must learn to accept the love a person gives you. Ingrates. All so many ingrates." She rose and dressed hurriedly. At the door she turned back.

"W-what about my pill?" the girl wailed.

"Do without, you ungrateful child."

Flora Belle returned in a few minutes. She carried a pair of manacles in one hand and a length of rope in the other. She cuffed the girl's hands and fastened the long hemp line to the connecting chain. The other end of the coil she strung through a pulley in the ceiling. All the while, the frightened, disoriented girl struggled and pleaded.

"What are you doing? I'll be good. I promise. Please don't leave me like this. All I need is a sugar pill. Only one, please. I'll be good."

"You'll love me like you should?" Flora Belle demanded craftily.

"Not that. Anything but that. It . . . it . . ."

"It sent a thrill through you, didn't it? Felt better

than anything you'd ever had before, right?"

"Yes . . . but . . ."

"And you refused me. You'll pay for that, yes indeed." Her task completed, Flora Belle hauled with all of her strength. The girl rose, painfully and against her will, until her toes barely touched the rough plank floor of the room. Then Flora Belle produced a whip.

The long lash curled out behind her and came whistling through the air. The leather bit into the tender flesh of the girl's back. Carefully controlled, it didn't break the skin, leaving only an angry red weal. The hapless prisoner cried out, then choked off her agony. Again the whip slashed the air and wrapped, curling, around her slender waist. The knotted tip struck her secret place and a howl burst past her tightly closed lips.

"How is it? How do you like what happens to girls who don't behave?" Flora Belle cawed while she plied the lash.

The agony served to awaken new avenues in the girl's mind. She suddenly grasped at an image and a name. Her name! Her name was . . . was . . . Rebecca. Yes, that was it. Rebecca. Rebecca Caldwell. More memory flooded in. Each fall of the flail let recollection in. Her uncle had caught her, put her here, wherever *here* was. Her name was Rebecca Caldwell and her uncle had imprisoned her. Oh, how wonderful to know your name . . . Rebecca . . . Rebec . . . Reb . . ." The flogging ended and Flora Belle placed a fat opium ball in her mouth.

Automatically she chewed and swallowed. Clarity and reality faded. Desperately she tried to hold on to that one precious fact. Her name was Reb . . . R . . . R . . . R . . .

* * *

. . . "Your name is *Sinaskawin*. That is what I call you and what others will know you by and what you will call yourself." Iron Calf glared down at the crouching girl.

Defiance flashed hotly in her eyes. "No, I am not an Indian and I will not be called by an Indian name."

"You are under my protection, you belong to me and you will obey me. You are *Sinaskawin*, White Robe Girl." Iron Calf declared arrogantly. He turned away and walked off through the Oglala village with the haughty gait of the Sioux warriors.

Desperately she looked up to her mother. Hannah Caldwell remained mute, stricken by fear and guilt. Dare she reveal to her daughter the frightful secret she had lived with these fourteen years? How could she. To even think of it was to conjure up horror beyond endurance.

"I will not," Rebecca muttered again. She saw the glazed look in her mother's eyes and realized that the woman had once more withdrawn into the protection of oblivion. She mustered her resolve. Never would she be called by that name. Never! . . .

. . . Numbness had replaced pain. She lay on her bed again, the world consisting of fuzzy outlines and insubstantial pieces of furniture that would suddenly lose shape and waver swimmingly for long moments before returning to the original form. The awful punishment had ended. Only twinges remained. She sensed someone else in the room and turned her head.

A small girl stood beside the room's only sturdy table. She indicated a tray of steaming food. "You're awake now. That's good. You need to eat."

"I . . . I want a pill."

"They aren't good for you. Eat first. Your supper is

128

getting cold."

"Sup . . . but I thought it was morning. It should be breakfast."

"Oh, morning was a long time ago. You were busy entertaining a gentleman friend then. At the noonin', too."

"Where . . . is . . . this . . . this place? And . . . wh-what is your name?"

"My name's Sue Ann. This is a . . . a bawdy house."

"Sue Ann. I like that name. Sue Ann . . . Sue Ann . . ." she repeated in a sing-song tone, like a litany. It gave her something solid to hold onto. "But . . ." Painfully the thought formed. The child looked so young and vulnerable. How did she, how did either of them get into a bawdy house? "How old are you, Sue Ann?"

"Twelve."

"And you . . . I mean, you *work* in this wretched place?"

"Oh, not like *that*, at least not yet. I do errands, clean rooms and help the girls." She examined the naked girl who rose from the bed on unsteady legs. "You're very pretty, did you know?"

"Thank you, Sue Ann. How . . ." her head pounded and thinking was a debilitating endeavor. "How is it you . . . you got here in the first place?"

"My folks died of a fever last winter. The old man who lived next to us took care of me for a while. I wanted to stay with him but he wouldn't hear of it. I even promised to be real good to him, take care of everything he needed. He said he didn't cotton to a filly young as me. I told him I was ready, could cook and sew and . . . and look after a man in every way. He brought me here and made some arrangement with Flora Belle."

"When was this?"

"Two days ago."

The drug-sodden girl turned desperate eyes on Sue Ann. "Then, maybe you know . . . what . . ." Confusion rose to choke her. "What is my name?"

Sue Ann giggled. "You must know that. Don't you? I mean, really?"

"No I don't. I don't." Tears of frustration leaked from under closed eyelids. "Please tell me."

"Why, that's easy. You're Rebecca."

"Rebecca," she said wonderingly. "Rebecca. And you're Sue Ann . . . Sue Ann . . . and Rebecca . . . Rebecca." She repeated the names to save them forever.

Suddenly the door burst open and Flora Belle entered, her face a mask of fury. "What is this? You haven't eaten yet, you naughty girl? Finish at once or no sugar pills for you. And as for you, you little gossip," she raged, rounding on Sue Ann. "I'll deal with you later. Get out. Get out! Can't you see she needs to freshen up for a gentleman caller?"

After the frightened girl scurried from the room, Flora Belle spoke again. "You've got a caller, dearie. He'll be up in a moment."

"But, I . . . I need another pill. The . . . the medicine will do me good. I have to have it!" she ended in a near-shriek.

"Perhaps half of one. Like before. Uh, do you remember your name now?"

Hope returned. "Oh, yes. It's Rebecca."

"Yes. Definitely. At least half of one," Flora Belle decided aloud, silently cursing Sue Ann for being a busybody. All their work. Oh, well, the opium would soon take care of that. She measured out a small dose and gave it to Rebecca.

Twenty minutes later, out in the hall, Ezekial

Caldwell turned from the spy hole, a lustful expression on his face. "She sure can come up with some wild positions," he grunted to Flora Belle Chase. "Lots of variety in that gal. Them Sioux must have really taught her a thing or two. You've done well, Flora Belle. How ever did you come upon this scheme?"

"Trade secret. Actually it was an old Chinkee-Chinaman. He worked for me at my house in New Orleans. He came to me one day and showed me the opium. 'Give me a girl fresh off the streets, some of my fellow countrymen can steal one,' he said. 'With this I will turn her out in three days.' And he did. I've been usin' it ever since."

"How long before this one is ready to work the floor?"

"Give me another day. Her time sense is destroyed. She thinks she has been here for weeks, doin' all sorts of fellers. Got her so doped she don't remember her name, unless someone like that little baggage I took in goes and tells her. Yes, I'd say by this time tomorrow, she can be put on the floor. Like that girl the China-man trained for me. She never left me."

"Which one of the present ones is it? I'm curious."

"Oh, none of these. Poor thing got to liking the poppy juice so much, kept needing more each day. Then one night she took a couple of balls and went to sleep. She never woke up."

THIRTEEN

Dust swirled in the air, strange considering the multitude of mudholes that filled the streets. Noise everywhere. Crowds of people jostled each other and talked at a raging pitch, making rude sounds, not listening to what others told them. And always hurrying through the streets of Denver. At first he felt amused. Then, as time went on, he found their hustle and bustle to be an irritant. His freshly shaven head itched, as did his armpits and crotch. White man's clothing restricted him, felt alien and uncomfortable. He walked on, determined to reach his destination with a minimum of discomfort.

Suddenly a man shouldered him roughly from behind. Lone Wolf's hackles rose. He wanted to spin and smash the rude man in the mouth. Among the Crow, as with most Indian people, such unsolicited contact was the ultimate insult. Lone Wolf curbed his anger, until the man spoke.

"Watch where you're goin', feller."

"Where *I'm* going?" Lone Wolf blurted. "You ran into me."

"Ain't the way I seen it, feller." The stranger balled one fist. "You want to walk on this street, you better stay awake." His sneer and slitted eyes telegraphed his punch.

Lone Wolf easily blocked the expected blow. In the same instant, he rolled his right shoulder and drove stiffened fingers forward into the man's solar plexus.

Air gusted from the belligerent man, rendering him meek and reasonable. In a quiet whisper, Lone Wolf reasoned with him. "Mister, were I you, I would work real hard at improving my manners. Shove me again and I'll wear your scalp on my belt."

The man stood gaping as Lone Wolf stalked off down the boardwalk.

"The U.S. marshal's office is right down the hall there," a young male clerk told Lone Wolf five minutes later in the Territorial government office building. "But there ain't anyone there."

"When will the marshal be in?"

"Who knows? He went off Raton Pass way to look into a dispute between some miners and the Mezkins living there. Best guess is he'll be back by Monday. You can check back then."

"Is there anyone . . . a deputy . . . ?"

"Nope. He took all his deputies with him."

"I . . . ah, thank you." Disappointed in the failure to fulfill his mission, Lone Wolf walked outside into the noisy, dusty confusion of Denver. He turned to his left and started toward a cafe he had eaten in that morning. Maybe a cup of coffee, with lots of sugar, would lighten his mood. A block down the street, a sudden altercation boiled out into the street.

Three men burst from a saloon, in the wake of a fourth, whom they had hurled through the batwing doors. Their victim, a small, mousey-timid man in his late thirties, landed in a mudpuddle. Mucky grime and decomposed manure smeared his white shirt and blue, pin-stripe vest. He raised his pinched face, spatters of filth on his thick-lensed spectacles.

"But I didn't even say anything to you," he protested in a squeaky voice. "Mister, I don't even know your name."

"It's Rudy Sellers, Sergeant, Colorado Volunteers. An' these boys is in my outfit, Deke Smith and Al Ruppe. Now that the introductions is over, we're gonna kick your ass," he ended in a harsh growl.

Rudy's name meant nothing to Lone Wolf, nor did the predicament of the unfortunate young man. Colorado Volunteers brought an instant response.

"My friend here," he nodded toward the man sprawled in the mudhole, "and I don't consider three against one fair odds."

"Butt out, feller, if you don't want to get tromped, too," Al Ruppe snarled.

"Oh, you're a brave one," Lone Wolf drawled sarcastically. "I'm totally petrified with fear." His hard knuckles, brought up from his waist without any warning, caught Al on the point of his chin.

His head snapped back, made contact with the clapboard wall of the saloon with a hollow sound, and rebounded. Al's eyes rolled up in his head and he went slack in the knees. Instantly the other two jumped on Lone Wolf.

Tensed for the attack, Lone Wolf took the swinging fists on his shoulders, rolling with each punch, then hammered his closed left hand down on the top of Deke Smith's head. Pain jarred up his arm, but his attack bore instant fruit.

Smith went down, a moan ripped from his throat. He didn't stay there long, though. In a blur of motion, the intended victim of these Chivington bullies rose from the mudhole and rammed into Deke. His small fists pounded a rapid tattoo on the larger man's chest. Deke recoiled from the assault, rammed his head against the upright of the saloon's balcony and bounced back in time to catch a punch in the mouth.

"I'll . . . drink . . . where . . . I . . . damn well . . .

134

please," the bespectacled townie grunted out, another fist to Deke's bloodied mouth with each word.

His vehemence amused and heartened Lone Wolf, who had his own problems with Rudy Sellers.

The Colorado Volunteer sergeant had stamina and bull strength on his side. Against these, Lone Wolf pitted speed and cunning. When Rudy charged him, he sidestepped, plowed a fist into the bigger man's kidney and kicked him hard in the crack of his buttocks. Rudy stumbled forward, bellowed with rage and came on again, awkward in his turn and first step.

Lone Wolf hooked a leg around Rudy's leading calf and cleaned him off his feet. Rudy landed in the mud-puddle, so recently occupied by his intended victim. He roared with fury and came up swinging wildly.

Lone Wolf batted aside the unaimed blows and stepped in close. He pummeled at Rudy's bulging midsection until the red-headed bully bent double. Rudy gagged and tried to suck in more air. Lone Wolf gave him no chance.

With both hands clasped, he slammed down on the citizen soldier's exposed neck. Rudy's body brought a loud, hollow thump from the plankwalk when he struck it, buck-teeth first.

"Hold it!" The voice from behind Lone Wolf crackled with authority.

Lone Wolf turned to see a barrel-chested man with widely bowed legs, encased in a pin-stripe suit. Long, lush arcs of a walrus mustache drooped around a hard, thin-lipped mouth. He wore a rakish bowler, a big Colt revolver . . . which he held steadily in his right hand . . . and a shiny star.

"Morning, Constable," Lone Wolf greeted the city lawman. "Sorry for the ruckus. These three attacked this gentleman and then went after me. I had no choice but to pacify them."

"Rudy Sellers attacking someone? I heartily doubt that, Mister. He's a respected member of John Chivington's militia. I don't know what your quarrel was about, but seems to me you must have been at fault. Better give me your name so I can get it right on the arrest report."

"Arrest?" The lawman nodded. "I'm . . . ah, my name is Baylor, Brett Baylor."

"Well then, Mr. Baylor, come with me. You are under arrest for assault."

Lone Wolf stared bleakly at the wall of his cell. The entire inner structure had been made of mud blocks, adobe the Mexicans called it. The building's outer shell was constructed of sawed pine slabs, three inches thick and twelve wide. Floor to ceiling iron slats formed the front of each of three cells. Only one other held an occupant. He had tried to make conversation with Lone Wolf, who ignored him until he shut up. Someone had used a spoon or belt buckle to carve initials and a date on one of Lone Wolf's adobe cell walls. From the distant office, Lone Wolf heard angry voices raised in argument.

"Now, damn it, Carl, you know a fistfight can't be considered assault. At least not here in Denver."

"All the same, I arrested him. Think of what John Chivington would say if we let some stranger come into town and kick hell out of three of his men and not do something about it."

"I don't care what Colonel Chivington thinks. That man is a fanatic, dangerous. You know that as well as I. I'm the justice of the peace here and I say we release this man, ah, Baylor."

"At least wait, Frank, until Chivington's militiamen

leave town. That's not too much to ask, is it?"

"In this case, it is. Think, Carl. Do you want people to say you're in John Chivington's pocket?"

"I'd rather be in his pocket than on his list of enemies."

Frank snorted derisively. "I still say to release Baylor."

"You're the judge. But let's wait until Chivington's men leave town."

"You make powerful enemies, friend," the disembodied voice came from the other cell.

Made curious by the conversation he had overheard, Lone Wolf spoke to his fellow prisoner. "How does anyone get that much power?"

"You mean our splendid Col. John Chivington? All you got to do is hate Injuns and make a lot of noise about it. There's always some who will join with you in making the world safe for the white man."

"You sound bitter. Or are you not a white man?"

"I am an Arapaho. At least on my mother's side. My father was a trapper, a mountain man. The winter nights get cold in these mountains . . . lonely, too. So my Pap up and traded off for an Arapaho squaw."

"I understand. I lived ten years with the Crow," Lone Wolf confided.

"It's not the same thing. Half-breeds are welcome in neither world. Whatever space we have we must make for ourselves."

"Tell me about Chivington."

"He is a menace. He came here some while back, started stirring people up about the Arapaho. There were some raids on two villages, a few people shot, but no way to prove for certain Chivington was behind that. In one, a reservation agent was killed. Those who back Chivington claim the Arapaho did that. Others suspect that those killers Chivington calls militia were responsible. Now there's trouble being stewed up for the Cheyenne. Again, Chivington is right in the center of it. Before long, something very bad is going to happen. You can count on that."

"Meanwhile, I sit in jail because Chivington has powerful friends."

"You've got it wrong, friend. Constable Kane considers Chivington too powerful to buck. You'll be out before suppertime, I'll bet."

"I've never been in a jail before. It's . . . too confining."

"Get used to it. That's all you can do."

"I never thought I could be so hungry," Rebecca Caldwell told the pretty young girl who stood beside the small table where a plate of food had been placed. Sue Ann put a hand on Rebecca's shoulder.

"That's more words than you've said since . . . since I've known you."

"I'm feeling much better now. And I remember my name. It's Rebecca," she said proudly. "Only . . . I do wish I had another sugar pill. I seem to have a bit of nerves."

Sue Ann pursed her mouth. "I . . . I don't think they are good for you. But all of the girls here take them."

"All of the girls? Where is this place?"

"The Mother Lode. But . . . but, I've told you before. It's . . . it's a bawdy house."

Sudden, fragmented memories flowed over Rebecca. Her stomach churned in revulsion at the remembered acts of depravity she saw imaged in her mind. Had she actually participated in . . . in such unspeakable things? The food tasted flat, unappetizing. Then another consideration came to her.

"H-how did I get here?"

"I don't know. I . . . I've only been here three days now."

"But, that . . . that's not possible." Rebecca looked around her wildly. It all seemed so confused. "We've talked before. It must have been days, weeks ago."

"Oh, no. That was only last night and today. Don't you . . . aren't you well yet? You seemed awfully funny before. And then they made me bring you all those meals. Oh, it's so confusing. Don't you *know* Rebecca?"

"I don't. Can't you see?" Unreality threatened to destroy her small hold on sanity. "Why would anyone want to do something like that to me?"

Flora Belle Chase entered through the narrow door. "Well, well, look at this. You've eaten right well, dearie. That's a good girl. How are you feeling?"

Rebecca put a slightly trembling hand to her cheek. "I'm all right . . . I . . . well it seems I have a bit of nerves."

"I've just the thing for you. A nice candy for your dessert. Take it down, dearie. Just a good old sugar pill, like before."

Desperately, Rebecca reached for it.

"That's a good girl. Are you going to be nice and put on your pretty new dress tonight, so you can work downstairs? If you do, there'll be some more of this wonderful candy waiting."

"I'll be good. I promise I will," Rebecca said urgently, already beginning to drift . . .

FOURTEEN

Marshal Kane let Lone Wolf out of the Denver jail early the next morning. Roosters trumpeted the coming dawn and the chill air whistled down the empty streets. Only a saloon swamper, on his way to work, and two teamsters, tending to their loads for a sunup departure, could be seen along the main thoroughfare. At the nearest cafe, he discovered he would have to wait an hour until they opened to get a cup of coffee to warm his chilled body. Boot heels sounded on the boardwalk behind him and the white warrior turned, expecting the worst.

"You're the feller who cleaned Rufus Sellers' plow?" a friendly voice inquired of him. "I heard that Marshal Kane was going to let you out this morning. I wanted to look you up and tell you not everyone in Denver is behind the high-handed activities of John Chivington."

"Well, ah, thank you, Mister . . . ?"

"Archer. Ted Archer. I didn't get your name."

"Brett Baylor," Lone Wolf replied, his white name still sounding foreign on his tongue.

"Nice to meet you, Brett. Come along. The dining room at the Palace Hotel is open. I'd like to buy you a cup of coffee."

"That's mighty kind of you, Mr. Archer."

"Please, make it Ted."

"I'm obliged, Ted. I've not been to the Palace."

Archer looked sourly amused. "It certainly beats our jail."

They walked off, Archer directing the way. A waiter with rolled up sleeves and gaudy red-and-black sleeve garters seated them at a small table, covered with a white tablecloth. He brought them steaming mugs of coffee and stood by, pad and pencil in hand.

"Breakfast, Brett? I'm going to have some."

"I suppose I should," Lone Wolf admitted reluctantly. "What Marshal Kane served looked like congealed hog swill."

"Steak and eggs for both of us," Archer ordered.

"Venison, buffalo or pork?" the waiter inquired.

"Buffalo for me," Lone Wolf replied, pleased by this prospect. Perhaps the white man's way wasn't all bad, he told himself.

"Oh, that's such a pretty dress," Sue told Rebecca when the older girl stepped shakily into the hallway.

Rebecca wore a skimpy dancehall costume of shimmering green material, with low-cut bodice, lots of black lace and a hem that covered only to her knees. She had a matching emerald feather in her hair, instead of a hat and her long black tresses had been swept upward to emphasize the rise of her cheekbones. Sue Ann reached out to touch the material.

"Oh, I hope I'll have one like that some day."

"I'm sure you will, Sue Ann," Rebecca responded. She felt awful. Flora Belle had allowed her only one of the dreaming pills that day. Her nerves vibrated like someone had rubbed her skin with a file. Her mouth tasted of ashes and a dull, persistent pain throbbed in her skull. She had been promised all of the medicine she wanted if she performed her duties properly. Confused, she asked about her duties.

"You're to entertain gentlemen callers, dearie," Flora Belle had informed her. "Like you've been doing for weeks now."

Weeks? The revelation stunned her. She had no way of knowing that only three days had passed since her capture by Tulley's gunhawks and her uncle's sentence that sent her into the brothel. Opium had robbed her brain of the conversation with Sue Ann which had revealed the awful hoax.

"How do I entertain them?"

Flora Belle had produced a lewd chuckle. "Why on your back, dearie. How else? Or sometimes on your elbows and knees, or with that pretty mouth of yours."

"But . . . you mean with just *anyone?*"

"Certainly. That's what we women do best, isn't it?" Her voice had changed then, grown hard. "Listen, dearie, around here it's a matter of no workee, no eatee. And particularly no sugar pills to take the pain away. You get down there on the floor and turn tricks or I'll take the lash to you."

Rebecca had wept after Flora Belle left, then freshened her face in cool water and dressed in the gaudy clothes provided. She knew her name, but had lost all other memories. Perhaps . . . perhaps she had always been a . . . a soiled dove? She had girded herself for the ordeal and now stood uncertainly at the head of the stairway. Flora Belle slipped up to her side.

"You'll use the name Yvette. For some damned reason, these horny buggers prefer girls with French names. Now go on out there and knock them dead."

Regally, in the best manner she could muster, Rebecca began to descend the stairs. The effect was astounding.

The music stopped and conversation died, only one loud, drunken voice holding sway at the bar. All eyes turned toward her and the hard-bitten miners and other denizens of Grub Stake stared, gape-mouthed at the enchanting apparition that seemed to float down toward them. When she reached the bottom riser, the spell broke.

"Whooie! Would you look at that!" one fuzzy-faced miner exclaimed.

"Purty as an angel," a companion agreed.

"Heavenly in bed, too, I'll bet," a gambler at the next table added.

Flora Belle drifted down to the landing and held up her hands for attention. "Boys, this is Yvette. She's new here and I want you all to give her a warm welcome."

"Yeah. But will she give us a warm welcome?" an unseen wit inquired.

A dozen men guffawed.

"She'll do that, all right," Flora Belle declared with certainty.

Self-consciously, Rebecca started toward the bar, a fixed smile on her pretty lips. She sought a wide empty space where she could arrange her thoughts, only to discover it filled rapidly at her approach.

"Let me buy you a drink, Miss Yvette," a gangling young miner offered.

A burly stamp-mill operator shoved the boy out of the way. "Get outta here, Sonny. This is man's work." He whipped off his hat and held it in nervous fingers. "Miss Yvette, I'd be right pleasured if you'd jine me for a drink. And then maybe we could sorta carry on the conversation in your room?"

Rebecca's lips trembled and she experienced a blind panic when her mind refused to provide the expected answer.

* * *

Matt Peterson stared blankly out the door of his shanty. Three nights now and no sign of Rebecca. Where had she gone? And why? They were to have dinner together the day following her introduction to banker Ross and Tom Allison. But she hadn't appeared. Had the fault been his? Had he said or done something to offend her? They were good together in bed. The best. Becky had seemed to enjoy it well enough. Her own hunger exceeded his, in fact. And she had achieved the satisfaction she sought, of that he was sure. Why, then, did she simply go away without any message or without seeing him again?

Could she have somehow been frightened off at the prospect of fighting so large a force as the Tulley gang? No, he told himself. From what he had heard, she had confronted nearly as large a band of outlaws before and bested them. Could she be looking for her friend who went to Denver? A momentary twinge of jealousy burned his heart.

Rebecca had explained about her companion, Lone Wolf Baylor. A captive of the Crow and, for ten years a warrior. They were not, Becky had assured him, lovers. Yet Matt wondered. Dismayed and, with nothing else to do, he decided on a stroll through the streets of Grub Stake.

Unconsciously his feet led him unerringly toward the brightly lighted front of the Mother Lode. At sight of it, the anger boiled up. His father had worked hard to build the saloon, sacrificed a great deal. Only the constant flow of gold, wrested from the surrounding hills and streams, repaid his investment. Hard working men were usually hard drinkers, too. His father had impressed that maxim on him often enough. It had proven true in the case of the Mother Lode. Within three months of opening, Matt's father had repaid his loan to the bank in Denver. Construction began on the fine house, the largest and most elaborately furnished in the entire town. After the death of his wife, Rolf Peterson had cared for his three children and seen them raised to adulthood. The elder two had married and left home. Matt remained at his father's side.

Everything had seemed to be going right. Then Tulley and his gang rode into Grub Stake and taken over. After his father's murder, Matt had went on living in the grand house, only to be physically ejected when Tulley announced that the small mansion was to be the residence of the man who would be the state legislator for the area. Matt had located a hovel, abandoned by a miner who had struck sand instead of gold. He moved in with what few possessions he could spirit away from his home. Yet, now he found himself compelled to go into the saloon to see what had been done since Tulley took it and, to salve his wounded pride over Rebecca's disappearance, drink a little whiskey.

As he passed through the batwings, the total difference struck him like a well aimed blow. Saloon girls lined the front and one side of the long bar, while others sat at tables or strolled the floor looking for men to entertain. Dozens of them. His father never countenanced prostitutes in his place. Now the reek of cheak perfume and the shrill peals of feminine laughter filled the smoky atmosphere. In one corner of the room, two burly miners with ham-sized forearms were engaged in an arm-wrestling contest. Three soiled doves shrieked support for their favorites, hovering over the sweating, straining men, full, lush breasts brushing broad masculine backs. A piano player, not his father's employee, but another, coal-black and shiny, with a bald head and two bright rows of white, tombstone-sized teeth, pounded the keys of the old upright, in vain competition to the noisy bustle of the barroom.

Matt looked for a space at the bar and headed over. His unease increased when he saw the small, close-set, pig eyes of the man behind the mahogany. They contrasted with the huge bulk of shoulders and thick-fingered hands that dwarfed the beer stein he was wiping dry. He looked up at Matt's approach.

"What'll it be?"

"Beer . . . no, make it a whiskey. Double."

"Dust, nuggets or hard cash?"

"Cash."

"Good." The barkeep smiled, revealing discolored teeth and increasing the aura of strength. "We don't get much of that here. Be sorta a change." He poured in a "fish-eye" shotglass and slid it in front of Matt. "Fifty cents."

Matt paid and took a long sip. The fiery liquid burned from the tip of his tongue to the bottom of his stomach. Rot-gut of the lowest order. He slid the glass back toward the apron.

"Get me some real whiskey, not this panther piss."

Bushy eyebrows rose over the pig eyes. "It'll cost you."

"Did I ask about that? Bring the bottle."

"I figgered on that. Only way we sell the good stuff."

When the liquor arrived, Matt tasted it and nodded approval. A soiled dove swayed her way up to him and draped an arm over one shoulder.

"Buy the lady a drink?"

"Sure. Why not? My bottle or the house swill?"

The hooker cast a quick glance over her shoulder toward the stairs, seeking Flora Belle. Reassured when she did locate the madam, she nodded toward Matt's fine Kentucky bourbon. "I'll take some of that."

146

While Matt poured, she continued. "You want to go upstairs with me?"

"I hadn't considered that," Matt answered honestly. Despite himself, he felt a stirring in his loins.

"I'll be good to you. That's a promise. We can have lots of fun."

"How much?" The stirring had become a rising lump of resurrected flesh.

"Two dollars. Five for all night."

"That sounds fair enough." Matt downed another shot of whiskey while his turgid organ became a large, insistent bulge in his trousers. Then the image of Rebecca Caldwell, naked, passed through his mind. He had to work hard to stifle the groan that wanted to escape from his throat. Rebecca. Where was she? He looked back at the jaded hooker.

She wore too much makeup, slabbed on like pancake batter, erasing her skin texture and no doubt hiding a multitude of unflattering wrinkles and sallow complexion. Could such a one spring his cock to life so easily, he asked himself.

The answer, obvious to him and the girl, was yes. Her eyes gazed downward and took in his readiness. Then she confronted him with a bold, starkly sensual stare.

"I see you're rarin' to go. Bring our bottle, honey. No need to waste any of that marvelous nectar." She caught at his hand.

Matt held back. Again the image of Rebecca taunted him. Only . . . only this time she seemed to be real and here in the same room.

Over the shoulder of the soiled dove, Matt saw another saloon girl. She had a burly miner by one hand and led him toward the stairs. She looked so much like Rebecca. Only she appeared a travesty of the beautiful girl he loved. Gaunt of face, hollow-eyed, her slender form starkly thin, she moved like an automaton. To Matt's eyes, her gestures were artificial, forced. She had a nervous little habit of jerking her head from side to side, as though in fear of something. This haunting ghost robbed Matt of his ardor. His throbbing penis went flaccid. Instantly the girl with him caught the direction of his attention and the effect.

"That's Yvette. She's new here. I can do a lot more for you than she can. C'mon, what do you say?"

"Yvette? When did she come here?"

"This is her first night on the floor. Let's go, big boy. From the looks of it, you've got enough there for two girls. If . . . if you like, I can arrange it so you can have both of us. Me an' Yvette at the same time. Would you like that?"

Matt thought a moment. He had never done that before. The idea showed promise. Then the similarity between the prostitute and his Becky taunted him again. He shifted a short way away from the girl.

"I . . . uh, think I'll wait until she's done. Let me think on it. Maybe we can all go together."

Hard Rock Mike opened his eyes to blackness. Then a door swung wide and a lighted coal-oil lamp approached. Were there doors in hell . . . or lamps? A slight figure was silhouetted behind the bright glow. Mike recognized the face the moment the man set down his light.

"You're awake," Doc Silver observed. He rubbed a long, soft-tipped finger against the bridge of his prow-like nose and leaned closer. "You lost a lot of blood, Mike. Who bushwhacked you? As if I needed to ask."

"I never saw them," Mike croaked from a dry throat. The doctor handed him a glass of water and he drank deeply. Feeling better he went on. "I've no doubt it was some of those bastards who work for Tulley."

"I thought so. *Oy*, that we should have such turmoil in our lives. I left a good practice in Vienna to escape bullies and brutes. Now they come here to Colorado to torment us. Those *schmucks* and what's to do about it?"

"We're tryin', Doc. At least we were before I got shot all to hell an' gone. How long have I been here?"

"A day. You need rest. Lots of red meat to give you strength. I have some soup. A venison stew and some hump meat."

At mention of the sweet, incredibly delicious buffalo hump, Mike's mouth watered. "Let me have some buffalo. The Injuns get some god-awful wounds and survive them. Some of the old timers insist it is because they eat buffalo. Now's as good a time as any to find out about it, eh?"

Doc Silver chuckled tolerantly. Modern science didn't allow for such homolitic remedies. Food, particularly meat, would strengthen the body so that the patient could survive until his system replenished the blood supply. That was all. Simple, really.

"Hump it is, if you're up to it." The doctor rose and departed, leaving the lamp for Mike.

Thoughts raced through his head. He felt weak, worn out and feverish. How long would it take for him to regain his feet? Was the girl, Rebecca, helping organize resistance to Tulley? Did she know what had happened to him? Did anyone? They had to move fast, before Tulley could consolidate his power. The Caldwell girl had been right in that. Only now . . . exhaustion overwhelmed him and he lapsed into a deep sleep.

Doc Silver awakened him two hours later. He held a

steaming platter of slices off a buffalo hump. The coarse-grained meat, so rich and savory in aroma and flavor, looked inviting to Mike. His saliva flowed freely. Eagerly he reached out for it.

"Na-na," Doc Silver cautioned. "I'm going to have to feed you this time. You're a lot weaker than you think, Mike. Next feeding, my son, Rubin, will do it. He's a good boy and will some day make a fine doctor."

Mike relented with bad grace. When a morsel of the succulent flesh lifted on a fork, Mike opened and accepted it gratefully. He chewed and the juices ran. So sweet. He could not distinguish the fiber from the fat. He swallowed and opened for more.

"Does anyone know I'm here?"

"Only the clothing merchant, Carstairs, and your banker friend, Ross."

"What about the Caldwell girl?"

"Funny, but no one has seen her in some time now. Young Matt Peterson mentioned it only yesterday."

The news stunned Mike. "You mean she has run out on us?"

"Who's to know? It might be, again it might not. All that is certain is that the lady is not around town. Now, you eat and rest and work at getting well. Let someone else do the worrying."

Matt Peterson waited expectantly for the return of the girl, Yvette. The more he thought on her the more convinced he was that something terribly wrong was going on in the Mother Lode. It couldn't be Rebecca. Yet, the resemblance went beyond coincidence. He had convinced himself of that. He desperately needed to know. The other girl, Marie, had grown bored with his evasive answers and idle remarks. She moved on to

150

solicit other customers.

She had little problem in doing that. The Mother Lode swarmed. And for a good reason. Tulley had closed down all competing establishments. If the miners, smelter workers and others of the town's male population wanted to drink, or have the companionship of young women, they had to take their custom to the Mother Lode. Matt's reflections were interrupted by the appearance of Ezekial Caldwell at his office door.

Some day you're going to get yours, Matt promised silently, eyes transmitting raw hatred at Ezekial. Some day soon.

Caldwell waved expansively at a favored customer and walked toward the bar, two henchmen beside him. A slight frown creased his forehead when he recognized Matt. Then he put on a professional smile and walked directly to where the young man stood.

"Ah, young Master Peterson. You have been well cared for, I trust?"

"Well enough," Matt returned coldly.

"We haven't seen you in the Mother Lode before. May I ask what the occasion might be?"

"I got thirsty."

Ezekial let go a short bark of laughter. "I like that one. I'll have to remember it for the future. 'I got thirsty.' Quite droll, really. I'd like to buy you a drink to show there's no hard feelings."

It took a teeth-gritting effort for Matt to control his fury. "I have a bottle, thanks."

"The Kentucky bourbon. Fine liquor, young man. Some of the best you will find on the frontier. Enjoy it in good health and with my compliments." Ezekial turned toward the barkeep. "Fred, refund Mr. Peterson's money. The bottle is on me."

"Yes, sir, Mr. Caldwell."

Ezekial adjusted his arm in the sling and moved through the crowd toward a faro layout against the far wall. He stood watching for a while, then gave a secret high sign to the dealer. Immediately, a big stakes winner began to lose. It wouldn't do for the house not to show a profit on everything. A big profit.

At the bar, Matt glowered at Ezekial Caldwell and returned to his whiskey. From the corner of his eye, he caught movement at the top of the stairs.

Wobble-legged, the miner who had gone upstairs with the Rebecca look-alike started downward. A silly, dreamy smile spread his lips wide and his eyes held a faraway look that advertised the success of his endeavor. Instantly, Matt hated him. He tensed then, waiting for the girl to appear.

Ten minutes passed and then she turned out of the upper hallway and began to walk down the stairs. Matt held his breath. She came closer and his nagging certainty grew. Yes. It had to be. But how and why? What circumstances could account for it? The girl reached the main floor and started toward the bar.

No doubt remained for Matt. It was . . . it was Rebecca!

FIFTEEN

Matt shook off his momentary shock at recognizing Rebecca. He moved along the bar to another open spot in her line of approach. When she drew near, he put on a big smile and nodded in a friendly manner.

"Hello. May I buy you a drink?" he asked in a voice he hardly recognized as his own.

"Why, ah, yes. That would be nice. Do you come here often?"

"This is my first time." Matt turned and signaled the barkeep. Their drinks arrived swiftly.

"I'm, ah, new here myself."

To Matt's ears, her voice had a strange quality, as though someone spoke in a dream. Pain burst in his chest, mingled grief and rage. What had they done to her? "Yes," he continued awkwardly. "Someone told me that." He knew there was only one place they could talk privately, so that he could try to get answers to the questions boiling up in his mind. "Would you . . ." he started uncomfortably, to be interrupted by Rebecca.

"Would you like to have a good time? We can go up to my room."

Fury ripped through Matt's breast. In his mind he saw an image of the miner, hands and face encrusted with ground-in dirt, who had gone upstairs with her. Had enjoyed her body. Hers . . . *his* girl! With an effort he calmed himself and forced what he hoped was an eager smile.

"Uh . . . h-how much is . . . is it?" Unaccustomed to brothels, Matt had little idea of the procedure. That he had to go through this with Becky made it worse.

"Two dollars for a good time. Five for all night. Dust, nuggets or cash."

"I've been waitin' for this all night. Here's the money, let's go." Rebecca took him by the hand and led him to the staircase. In the upper hallway, Matt placed an arm protectively around her shoulders. "It's going to be all right now."

"Huh? Wha . . . what do you mean?"

"Where's your room?"

"That one." Rebecca pointed to a thin panel of cheap, warped pine.

Inside, Rebecca immediately began to undress, an easy operation in her one-piece costume, equipped with the latest French invention, the zipper. Her gorgeous body, thinner now, revealed itself to Matt. He stared in hurt and amazement. God, she was lovely. For a moment, his resolve faltered. Then he forced himself on.

"Rebecca, we've got to get you out of here."

"Love first, then talk, big boy. And I bet you are a big boy." She reached out her hand for the money.

The agony of his heartbreak twisted in Matt's chest. Before he could try to press his argument, Rebecca reached out and seized his flaccid penis. Her deft fingers began to manipulate it and, despite the urgency he felt to help the girl, Matt found himself responding. Blood coursed and his maleness stiffened. Then Rebecca freed his belt and opened his trousers. Her eyes widened when his throbbing shaft popped into view.

"My, you *are* a big one," she cooed.

"Rebecca, Rebecca, listen to me. We've got to make a plan."

"How did you know my name? My real name?"

"I knew you . . . before you came here. Now, let's talk sense while there's time."

"Unh-uh. Love first, that's the house rules. Come with me . . ." she started for the bed.

His mind reluctant, his body burningly willing, Matt followed her to the creaking wooden frame and thin, soiled mattress. She faced him and brought her warm, passionate body tightly against his. Tingles of the old magic sped through Matt's flesh. He wanted her. Oh, God, yes, he wanted her.

"How do you like it?" Rebecca asked in artificial sweetness.

"Oh, Becky, Becky . . . I . . . Any way, any way you will enjoy." He suddenly felt miserable again. How many times had she asked that question since she disappeared? Of how many men? She smiled sweetly at him and lay back on the disreputable bed linen. Slowly, sensuously, she spread her legs.

"Is this all right?" she inquired in a little-girl voice.

In a wave of longing, Matt's passion overwhelmed him and he came to her with eager abandon. His massive penis ached from a magnificent erection and he longed to plunge it deep into her beckoning pleasure palace. He hovered over the girl on the bed and placed the sensitive tip of his manhood between her pert, upthrust breasts. Slowly he drew it down the silky length of her, thrilling to the sensations he knew delighted them both.

"None of that foolin' around," Rebecca admonished in a thickened voice. "It's the rules. You do your stuff and that's that. Unless this is for all night."

"Then it's for all night." Matt worked diligently to

kindle her ardor, but she failed to respond. Her eyes were glassy, distant, her body lax and unmoved by his practiced foreplay. At last, consumed by his own needs, he entered her.

She was barely moist enough to receive him. Her hips thrust mechanically and she rolled her eyes in simulated pleasure. "Oh, honey, that's great," she moaned, her words flat and lifeless.

Ice touched Matt's heart. They had made her into a machine. A vegetable-like receptacle for countless, impersonal peckers. How tragic, he thought. And how spiritless our lovemaking, which had been so good before. As a kid he had loped his mule to better effect than this produced. What did other men see in such creatures. With a sudden burst of guilt, he realized he had been condemning his Becky. How had this happened?

Dutifully, all hope of joy destroyed, he worked his way to completion. After he withdrew, he lay at Rebecca's side. "Now, let's talk."

"If you want," she responded listlessly. Idly one hand reached out to a square tin box on the night table. She opened it and took out a small, sticky brown ball. They were less than half the size of the ones she had been given before, but they did help get through the . . . the gentlemen she had to entertain. Even a little escape was better than none.

Matt saw the concoction and recognized it instantly. His firm hand whipped through the air and slapped the deadly drug from her grasp. It struck the floor and rolled a short distance. Now he knew how they had turned her into something . . . less than human.

"My pill!" Becky cried out. "Why did you do that? I . . . I have to have it." Automatically she reached for another.

Again Matt lashed out, this time knocking the small

container from her hand. "No. Don't you know what that is, Becky? It's . . . opium. From the dream poppy of China. It's . . . it's why you're here, like this. You must stop taking them, grow strong and able to escape. Your uncle has done this. Made you a prisoner. A horrible kind of prisoner."

"My . . . uncle?"

"Ezekial Caldwell. Don't you remember the name?"

"I . . . I sort of do. Sometimes, in the nice dreams the pills bring there is a man named Ezekial. Only . . . only he's cruel and does awful things."

"The same man in real life. Becky, you have been badly used. I have to find a way to get you out."

"But if he's my uncle . . . ?" Rebecca countered, returning to the previous subject with the single-minded stubbornness of a drug addict. "Why would he do this to me?"

"You said it yourself. He is an evil man. Do you remember Jake Tulley? Bitter Creek Jake Tulley?"

"N-no. Is he involved in this?"

"Oh, yes, very much so. At least I think he is. That's why you have to stop taking the opium balls. They kill your soul, then your body. Oh, my darling, do it. Do it for me.

"Who . . . who are you?"

Matt fought back the momentary stab of pain her words brought. She was not herself, he cautioned his seething emotions. "I'm Matt. Matt Peterson. Oh, don't you remember anything, Becky?"

"Matt? That's a nice name. I like to know names. But . . . you said this was your first time here."

"It is. I knew you before. Before your uncle somehow captured you and put you in this place. Try to remember. And please stop taking the pills."

Rebecca raised trembling fingers to her gaunt, hollow-cheeked face. "I'll try. I promise I will, Matt

Peterson. But . . . I get so sick when I don't have them. I have a sore stomach and my head throbs. Can I . . . can I take one when it gets too awful?"

"Yes," Matt reluctantly agreed. "But only then. And try each minute of the day to make it longer between pills. You will have to be careful, though," he advised. "Ezekial and Flora Belle will be keeping a watch on you. You'll have to dispose of them somehow so that they think you are taking all they give you. Can you do that, dearest?"

"You are so nice to me, Matt Peterson. You call me nice things. Why do you do that?"

"Because . . . because we were lovers."

"But, I've been here ever so long a time. How did you remember me?"

"It's only been . . ." Matt paused, wondering how to give her the truth without it having a negative effect on her. "You disappeared three days ago. Four tomorrow morning."

Rebecca blanched. "Only . . . four days? It can't be. I had so many meals, so many nights of sleep and . . . and the men they brought to me. I took my pills like a good girl and the days just rushed by. I'm sure it's been . . . weeks. Yes, weeks since I came here. I'm sure . . . I'm . . . No. I'm not sure of anything."

"You can be sure that I want what's best for you. That and only that. I will work on a plan and come back as soon as I can. Meanwhile, stop the opium and get ready to escape from here. I know you can do it."

Matt took her tenderly into his arms and kissed her with fervor. Rebecca's eyes popped open in a startled flash of memory. These lips, the same wonderful lips she had felt before, somewhere. Oh, yes, she would be safe with Matt. Safe and away from this awful place.

* * *

Bright yellow light streamed from kerosene hurricane lamps on the front of the Peterson mansion. Along the short drive *flambeaux* flickered red-orange. A small, closed carriage drew up at the portico and the driver's assistant dismounted to open the door.

Dapper in a maroon frock coat with black velvet facings, soot-gray trousers, the bottoms stylishly pegged, short, dark beaver hat, English saddle boots and spats, Roger Styles climbed from the interior and stood martially erect, stretching surreptitiously to ease the kinks of his long journey. A moment later, the front door opened and Jake Tulley stepped out.

"Roger!" he greeted affably. "Welcome to your new home. Do you like it?"

"It will do," Styles replied slightly disdainfully. He had long been adept at keeping inferiors in line. "For Grub Stake. The road is impossible. Our coach barely scraped through the trees. I'm in need of a brandy."

"All ready and waitin' for you. Teamsters brought in a wagonload of your stuff early this morning. Come on in." Jake led the way, with Roger following. Styles sniffed disdainfully at the air, redolent of smelting ore, and relaxed only after he and Jake had seated themselves in the small drawing room.

"What's the news?" Jake asked expectantly.

"Everything is going well in Denver. Has the election been announced?" At Jake's nod, he went on. "Good. I expect to make at least one campaign speech to these dullards before the voting. Matter of form, you know. Now, about that brandy?"

Jake turned to Clyde Morton. "Bring us both a brandy. The good stuff from Mr. Styles' stock."

"I ain't no servant," the young gunslinging punk muttered under his breath.

"Do as I say, or I'll kick your ass up between your shoulder blades," Jake growled back.

Once Morton had departed, Roger went on. "Our prospects look even better. We elect Wellington sheriff and there's no local pressure. As far as concern in Denver, you can forget that. We spread a little money around and put the arm on those who object and we can get away with wholesale murder if we want. When Colorado is a state, there'll be no more U.S. marshal to contend with. By the way, the one we've got is a bastard. All rules and strict enforcement. There's something else . . . strictly between you and me . . ." Roger paused as Clyde Morton returned with a tray, two glasses and a dusty bottle of premium brandy.

"How many times do I have to tell you to dust off those jugs?" Jake complained.

Morton took on a sour expression but remained silent. He used the tail of his shirt to clean the brown glass bottle, pulled the cork and poured. He handed one to Styles, then Jake.

"That's all, Clyde. You may go." Jake told him imperiously.

Morton departed with a hard slam of the door. "Ain't no fucking servant," he snapped on his way out.

"What's this secret you got, Roger?"

Styles allowed himself a small, smug smile. "There's a shipment of gold leaving Denver next week. An army payroll on its way to the Dakota Territory. It will pass close by here. Close enough to make it worth your while to intercept it. We would be ahead by a hundred thousand dollars."

"A hun . . . Lordy, that's real money, Roger." His eyes narrowed suspiciously. "You making a present of it to us?"

"Less my usual share . . . fifty percent."

Jake smiled, relaxed. He had instantly suspected trouble if Styles had not demanded his lion's share.

Now greed shone in his eyes. "Even at that, we'll make a killin', Roger. I swear this here Colorado's one big gold mine. So far, Ezekial's brought in a bit better than eight hundred dollars a day, most of it in dust and nuggets. The scale is rigged and we discount for hard cash. That way we make damn near double profit on dust. Flora Belle's whores are working out well, too. There was only a few chippies at a dance hall down the street before. I swear these miners would fuck a snake if someone held it still for them. The gambling is going smoothly, too. There's no place to go for liquor, women or cards but the Mother Lode. So everything out there we're takin' in."

"I'm pleased to hear that, Jake. Your ability to organize something beyond a stage or bank robbery is encouraging. Yes, I think our future is secure." Styles paused a moment, eyes narrowed as he changed the subject.

"Any word about that niece of yours?"

"No. None. An' no sign of her, either."

"The less heard from that quarter, the better, eh?"

"You can say that again, Roger. Though I would like to get my hands on that bitch. Plank her good then finish her off. More brandy?"

Darkness enveloped most of Grub Stake. The only lights came from the area around the Mother Lode and one large house on a back street. Lone Wolf cautiously skirted the small village, still seeking some trace of Rebecca. When he reached the outlying area, at the place they had agreed to rendezvous, he had found no sign to indicate she had been there watching for him. He waited until darkness fell and moved in toward town. He had found nothing and no one who could help. Now he decided to enter the streets. He had been worried about her since he started back from his fruitless trip to see the marshal.

One deputy had returned on Monday. A real shooting war had developed down in the Raton Pass country. Mexican sheep men and American settlers had gone at each other with a vengeance. The marshal and his men would be tied up for some time to come, the young lawman had told Lone Wolf. He would, the assurance came, look into the situation in Grub Stake the moment peace had been restored to Raton Pass. Conscious of the building danger in Grub Stake, Lone Wolf decided to head back. Perhaps something could be done in the meantime to put a kink in Tulley's plans. Lone Wolf left his horse in the pole corral that served the community as a livery. He decided against the Mother Lode. Even without his distinctive hair cut, some of Tulley's men might recognize him. Quietly he slipped down an alley and turned onto the side street where lights blazed from a large, two-story house.

Lone Wolf watched from the shadow of a gnarled old pine. Across the street, the light night breeze clattered through the small, spade-shaped leaves of a row of aspen trees, saved no doubt when the town had been laid out. He saw the silhouettes of several men against the closed blinds, though no one came outside. He crossed over and made his way between two houses.

At the rear, he again made careful observations, seeking to discover any sentries posted there. Instinct told him his enemy waited inside. Down the block a dog barked and a muttered curse followed. An owl hooted mournfully and made a swooping dive from its limb to snatch a mouse that scurried from the open doorway of a coal shed. A cloud covered the moon and Lone Wolf used its protection to make a short dash to the shed. He tensed, his senses finely tuned. The air brought him the scent of tobacco smoke. Footsteps crunched on gravel near the carriage house and he eased back into the shadows. A man approached. He paused near the coal shed and relieved himself. With a satisfied grunt, the sentry moved on. Lone Wolf had his answer.

Tulley, or someone else important, had to be inside. Could it be Roger Styles? It would be nice to have all their enemies in one place. A quick, easy kill. All he had to do was find Rebecca. Stealthily he moved to the side of the house and crept along until he reached a lighted side window. Voices came indistinctly from inside.

"It bothers me that she hasn't put in an appearance," Roger Styles admitted to Jake Tulley. "Are you sure there has been nothing that would indicate the Caldwell girl is in the area? She was supposed to be burning up the road, dead on our trail, remember?"

Jake thought a minute. "Well, there was one thing. It coulda been. Some of my boys disappeared. They showed up a couple of days later, all shot to hell. That and a long way from where they were supposed to be the day they dropped out of sight. It could have been miners done it, then again, it might be her. Damnit, I just can't figger that one out. Why's she so set on comin' after me and my boys? We didn't do nothin' all that terrible to her. An' Ezekial and Virgil bein' kin. Her shootin' Virgil down was cold. I mean, it's terrible times when family starts doin' for family like that."

"Tell me some more about these men who were killed."

"Hell, there ain't much, Roger. That's the problem. They was shot full of holes and left out in the trees. No blood around, so it's my guess they weren't done in here."

"Did anyone from around here do any talking?"

"Nope. None a'tall. I sent some men out under Luke to rough up a few miners, but he came back empty. Oh, that trouble with Mike Hoxsey, the troublemaker. Well, when I got back I found out he was taken care of right proper. No more worry from that direction."

"That's reassuring. Now, I brought along a new man for you. He's waiting out in the hall. Name's Lacey. 'Trapper' John Lacey."

"What's he like?"

"Fast with a gun. Pure leashed lightning. I want him here through the election. Then he will go to Denver with me to help administrate my office."

"Ya mean he's had schoolin'?"

"A lot of it. But his sharpest quality is his gunhand."

"Bring him in, I'd like to meet him."

Roger rose, stepped to the door and put his head out into the hall. "John, would you come in a moment, please?"

A man of medium height, in a linen duster, a dark suit visible underneath, entered the drawing room. He carried an expensive beaver hat in his left hand, a pair of neatly folded gloves clutched between two fingers. Rings sparkled on three digits, the diamond settings large and gaudy. He affected a pencil-line mustache and glossily slicked back black hair. Flat, expressionless gray eyes took in both men. A bulge under the left side of his duster indicated a revolver, worn up high, perhaps tucked into his belt.

"You wanted me, Mr. Styles?"

"Yes, John. This is Jake Tulley. You will be working with him until the election. Jake . . . Trapper John Lacey."

"Howdo. You ever, ah, heard of me, Lacey? Bitter

Creek Jake Tulley," the outlaw chief inquired anxiously.

Lacey's dead eyes took on a distant glaze. "A bank robber and highwayman of decidedly inferior quality, operating in northeastern Nebraska. Do I have it right?"

Tulley bristled. "Now, see here . . ." He stopped when Roger raised a restraining hand.

"Nothing to get upset about, Jake. John's only making a little joke. Actually he told me in confidence he looked forward to meeting you. Isn't that right, John?"

"Oh, yes. Of course, I would like to obtain firsthand knowedge of rattlesnakes and the bubonic plague, too."

"Does he always talk so damn funny?" Jake inquired.

Lone Wolf had heard enough. Apparently no one knew where Rebecca had disappeared to. He slipped quietly away from the window. At the corner of the building he paused until another cloud covered the moon, then started around to where he had approached the house.

He walked directly into two of Tulley's gunslicks.

"Hey!" "What?" They shouted out their surprise in unison.

Lone Wolf reacted instantly. He shoved one to the side and drew his hunting knife. His sudden attack did not come fast enough, though.

The barrel of a revolver smashed into the side of his head and he dropped to the ground, dizzied and weak beyond the ability to defend himself.

"Who the hell is he?"

"I don't know," the second hardcase replied. "Let's get him inside to Jake. He'll tell us what to do."

"Well, I'll be a son of a bitch!" Jake Tulley exploded

a few seconds later. He looked at the groggy figure on the Persian rug of the drawing room with wide eyes. "He's done rid himself of that silly hair-do, but I'll swear this is that white Injun who rode with Rebecca Caldwell. If he's here, then by damn it means the bitch can't be far away. Where'n hell is she?"

"I . . . I don't know what you mean," Lone Wolf responded.

"Smack him in the nuts with a boot," Jake ordered one of the sentries. "Maybe that'll loosen his tongue."

The outlaw gleefully complied. Lone Wolf suppressed a groan, though he could not prevent his body from doubling in agony, hands clutching at his savaged testicles.

"Where is she?" Tulley repeated.

Lone Wolf remained silent.

"Shit! She's either here already or coming along behind him. Chain him up in the coal shed, boys. Let him sweat it out for a while. In the mornin' we'll ask him a few more questions."

Fury beat through the pain. To be shackled like an animal! Lone Wolf raged impotently as the men dragged him from the room and confined him in the low-roofed shed.

SIXTEEN

For Matt Peterson, time passed slowly, agonizingly so, over the two days that followd his discovery of Rebecca Caldwell in the Mother Lode. He had been beset with ample to occupy his hours. Primary on the list, his constant struggle to keep the committee together and plan some form of resistance to Jake Tulley and the newcomer, Roger Styles. Styles was a dandy, damn near a sissy in Matt's way of seeing it. The announcement that he would be the candidate for the provisional state legislature from the Grub Stake area had angered nearly everyone in town. Hot words passed between Styles and the citizens of Grub Stake. The notorious gunslinger, Trapper John Lacey could always be found looming in the background wherever Styles went. It only complicated matters for Matt. He wanted to return to the saloon and shoot a way out for Rebecca and himself. Reason and caution prevented him. He knew it would take time to heal her and the only person who could accomplish her release from drugs was herself. He had to give her the chance.

While he did, he went from one person to the next, plotting, making sure of a large, hidden supply of ammunition and spare arms. In the process, he learned that Hard Rock Mike had survived the ambush that Tulley's gunhawks bragged about. He had been hidden at Doc Silver's place, a half mile out

167

of town, there to recuperate from his wounds. Already, on the afternoon when Matt went there, the feisty miner argued with his doctor about when he would be able to join the others in fighting Tulley.

"Now, dang it, Doc. I'm well, you hear? Well enough to handle a Winchester or throw a stick of dynamite at those . . . what'd ya call em?"

"You will do as your doctor orders," Doc Silver had commanded in a tone that prevented dispute. Untrained in subtleties, Mike's ear failed to interpret the nuance.

"I'm fit as can be. Why, I'm so healthy that my pecker even gets stiff again. Let me up, Doc."

"No. If you try, I'll pump you so full of laudanum that you'll sleep for a month."

Mention of the opiate medicine struck a chord with Matt. "Doc, I have a question."

"Go ahead. Free medical advice is something a doctor expects people to ask for."

"If a person had been given opium, lots of it, over a period of three days, how long would it take to get them off the effects and back to normal?"

"That depends on how strong the person's mind was. How much willpower they had. Doing it the slow way, with a bare minimum of the drug to ease the worst pains, I would say two to five days."

Matt produced a bleak expression. "I don't know if I have that long."

"This is for you?" Doc Silver blurted. "You don't . . . look like an addict."

"No. It's not for me. It's . . . I'd better wait and work it out first."

He left in a gloomy mood, the joy at finding Mike well on the way to healing dimmed by the doctor's words. He couldn't, he simply couldn't leave Becky in that foul place a moment longer than necessary. He spent all the next day brooding over it. By the time evening came, he knew he would have to check for himself. He dressed, tucking a small .38 caliber Remington New Line No. 3 into a special pocket sewn inside his vest, checked to see the round butt pistol didn't reveal itself through his clothing, then left his shanty for the Mother Lode.

Shrill feminine laughter came from inside the saloon. Smoke rolled out over the curved tops of the batwing doors in a steady stream. Men shouted and swore, and Matt could hear the tinkle of glassware and bottles. Inside he could not locate Rebecca. Visions of her in bed with some sweaty miner who bathed perhaps twice a year, who grunted and panted out his lust on her body, filled Matt's mind with torment. He stood at the bar, fidgeting like a small boy who has to use the outhouse. The barkeep came over.

"If you're lookin' fer Yvette, the one you went with last time, she don't come on the floor for another twenty minutes."

"Uh . . . uh, thanks." Relief washed through Matt's body, making him weak in the knees. "She . . . she's sure some gal."

"Big money maker," the apron agreed.

The observation made Matt boil. He flushed steadily. "Give me a beer."

"Comin' up."

A large schooner sailed down the bar toward him, trailing a wake of foam. It hove to precisely at his hand. Matt closed fingers around the thick stem and raised the fish-bowl glass to his lips. He found the beer cool and heady tasting. The mountainous area was rife with underground streams. His father had built the Mother Lode over one, put in a deep cellar and used the frigid water to cool his potables before bringing them up to the bar. Ezekial Caldwell, it seemed, had had sense enough to continue the system. Matt killed time by looking around at the men in the saloon.

He knew most of them by name. Had considered them friends as well as customers of his father's saloon. Now, with Rebecca a prisoner in the bordello upstairs, they had become enemies. Five miners played poker at a table in the far corner. Near the potbelly stove, cold now in summer, a faro dealer worked his layout. His three customers looked bored and defeated. Two trappers stood at the far end of the bar, swapping lies about how good their take of pelts had been the previous season. Everything seemed entirely normal. Like when his father had owned the place. But how could it be, with Becky captive upstairs? Becky . . . Becky . . .

"Yvette!" he shouted joyously when she appeared at the head of the stairs.

Two of the younger miners whistled and waved arms to try to attract her attention. She looked little changed from two days ago. Her condition disturbed Matt. Surely she hadn't slipped back under the influence of the drug? He prayed not. She ignored most of the rowdies and walked directly to the bar. A quick look around gave everyone a blank expression. Matt walked up to her, eyes light with expectation and hope.

"You look mighty familiar, honey," she told him. "Have I seen you before?"

"I was in the other night."

"To see me?"

"Right."

"Did you like what you saw?"

"You bet. That's why I'm back," Matt added for the bartender's benefit, "rarin' to go. What say we

170

head upstairs, darlin'?"

"Say, you're in a hurry. No time to buy a lady a drink?"

"I got somethin' here that can't be put off much longer." Matt made a slight gesture toward his crotch. To his dismay, he found he had spoken the truth. His manhood had begun to swell to eager fullness.

"Then, let's go, lover. I've got just the place to put it."

Upstairs, Rebecca led the way to her crib. "Two dollars, big man," she announced before closing the door.

"Here's a five dollar gold piece for the whole night."

The portal closed and, from down the hall, Flora Belle nodded in satisfaction. That one would make the house a fortune.

Immediately that they had privacy, Rebecca threw her arms around Matt's neck and pressed her cheek against his chest, deep sobs bursting from her. "Oh, Matt, my own dear Matt. Thank you for that. I . . . you see, I am a lot better. I remember you now. Know what . . . what we had together. Oh, how awful this place is. I want to kill them all. Let me get my hands on Uncle Ezekial and I'll shred him, I'll skin him alive, feed him to the crows, put him on an anthill."

"Now, now. Take it easy. How do you feel . . . I mean really feel?"

"Better. Oh, so much better. I don't use . . much of the opium. Very little really. It . . . it hurts most of the time, but each day I get stronger and memories returned. Oh, I feel so ashamed." Suddenly she released a nervous giggle. "How could a girl who's spent five years in a Sioux camp feel shamed to be in a brothel? At least that's what a proper white lady would say."

"I feel greatly relieved, Becky. You're starting to

171

talk like your old self."

"Oh, Matt, there's something we must do. I have a plan for the escape. But we have to take someone along. Sue Ann Marshal. She's only twelve. If she stays here much longer, I'm afraid of what will happen to her."

"Does she want to go?"

Rebecca frowned, thinking that over. "I'm not too sure she does. She's . . . she's very advanced in her attitudes for her age. Looks forward to wearing a dress like mine and working the floor. She seems to find nothing wrong with what's done up here. Wants to be a part of it. Flora Belle has let her watch a few times, through peepholes, she's told me. Says it makes her itch. But, Matt, she is so innocent. She has no idea how awful it is, what . . . what goes on up here. We have to save her. She started me back to reason. Even before you came in. Kept telling me the candy pills were no good for me. And once . . . oh, I don't remember when it was . . . she told me my name."

"That was important?"

"Oh, yes. You have no idea. I didn't know who I was, no name at all, except in the dreams the opium gave me. Now, I'm mad and I want to fight. Can we do it tonight."

Matt hesitated. "I . . . hadn't planned it that way. I wanted to give you more time to build your strength and come out of the dream world the opium put you in. But . . ."

"Oh, please say yes. It's important. Once I don't have it around tempting me, I'll get over the drug so much faster. And . . . I'm afraid for Sue Ann and me. Flora Belle is an animal. She tried to force me to . . . oh, never mind. That's for some other time. I'll talk to Sue Ann, get her ready. There is a back stairs to the place. Why, you should know that. After all, your father built this saloon."

Matt felt overjoyed. Memory seemed to be flowing back to Rebecca at a marvelous rate. Maybe they *could* work the escape tonight. He blinked, realizing that she had gone on talking.

"There's a back stairs and no guard on the top floor. Only a swamper who cleans out the slop jars and brings towels to the girls. He has a gun, but I figure we can take it away and knock him out. Then down the stairs, out the back door and away through the alley."

"What if Flora Belle discovers us in the act?"

Ice tinged her words and countering fire burned in Rebecca's eyes. "I'll take a lot of pleasure in killing her."

"All right. We'll do it." Matt decided in an instant. "You find out about the little girl. I'll make sure we have horses for a getaway."

"No. We'll walk away to your place. It will attract less attention in the event someone sees us. I can't wait. Oh, dearest, I can't wait."

"It is the only way. Don't you see that?" Rebecca told Sue Ann half an hour after Matt left her. "My memory is returning. I know who I am and why I was put here. This is a prison. No matter how glamorous you think it is, it is still a prison. Think, Sue Ann. Do you really want this sort of life?"

"No-no, I suppose not. It's only that . . . Flora Belle said she was my guardian now. That I had to do as she wished. That . . . left me little hope of anything else. Do you really mean it that we can leave and . . . just never come back?"

"Yes, dear. You will be free, so will I. There are people here, good people, who will care for you."

"Then . . . I want . . . to . . . go," Sue Ann decided.

The door burst open. Flora Belle stood in the opening, her face rouged with anger. "What are you doing here, little Miss? And where's your all night customer, Yvette?"

Rebecca stared coldly at the madam. "He went downstairs for a bottle of whiskey. Said we would make a party of it," she lied evenly.

"Well, tend to your knittin', dearie. Behave yourself and there'll be another tin of candy for you." Flora Belle switched her gaze to Sue Ann, her features softening, voice becoming dulcet. "Come with me, dear Sue Ann. There's something I want you to see, to do. You'll like it, I know."

A warning sounded deep inside Rebecca's mind. Vague images shifted and turned and she felt reassurance from the .38 Remington that Matt had left with her. Not as reliable a weapon as her Baby Russian, but it would do. She wanted Sue Ann to stay, but knew their plan depended upon Flora Belle's belief that she had a man spending the night with her. Reluctantly, the small girl walked toward the open door.

When she neared, Flora Belle placed an affectionate arm around her thin shoulders. The disturbing images passed through Rebecca's mind again. Blurred by the long bout with drugs, they made no sense. Yet something urged her to look further into this. She made certain of her revolver, then waited until she felt the hall would be empty. Quietly she opened her door and peered both directions. No one. Rebecca took a deep breath and went along the hall toward Flora Belle's room.

When she reached her destination, she saw first off that the latch had not caught securely. Carefully she eased the door open a crack. The opulent suite she saw beyond the threshold contrasted starkly with the narrow, shabby rooms occupied by the brothel's inmates.

An office-sitting room opened off the doorway, the bedroom behind it. From there, Rebecca heard Flora Belle's voice, the coarseness gone, replaced by a tone of affection and friendliness.

"My, how you are filling out, Sue Ann. The food must agree with you."

"I . . . I know I eat a lot, but I'm always hungry. I don't want to be a burden," the small girl answered defensively.

"Stuff and nonsense. You're no burden. I only meant that you look healthy. I'm curious. Would you . . . as a favor to me . . . take off your clothes?"

"Oh, but . . ."

"Now, now. Nothing to worry about. There's only us girls here. Take off your dress, dear." A note of command had crept back into Flora Belle's voice.

Clothing rustled and an ugly image of Flora Belle disrobing at the side of her bed flashed through Rebecca's mind. She tensed.

"Ah, that's it. Now your shift. I want to make sure you are filling out in all the right places."

Rebecca's senses whirled in a morass of revulsion as she recalled the madam's attempt to force her attentions on her own drugged body. She had to do something. But what? Clearly she could see the escape plan falling to ruin if she revealed her presence here. Flora Belle would be furious, suspicious of her and would certainly lock her in her room. Rebecca gritted her teeth and took hold of her flighty thoughts. No more than she could abandon her hope of freedom, she could not let anything happen to Sue Ann. If anything . . . worse went on, she would have to interfere, she vowed. All she could do now was wait and remain silent.

Flora Belle Chase reclined against a pile of pillows on the small couch in her bedroom. Her breathing roughened and she felt the heat spreading from her loins as she gazed longingly at the naked girl in front of her. No stranger to this sort of love, she let her memory slip back to that time long ago in St. Louis.

Her parents had promised her piano lessons and, when an attractive young woman moved into the neighborhood and put out a shingle advertising music instruction for refined young girls, she had been sent there. Flora Belle had been an astute student, progressing rapidly. The day came when Helen Smithers had rewarded her perfect execution of some difficult scales with a hug and a kiss on the lips. Flora Belle had returned the offering with ardor.

From then on, Helen had taught her more than five-finger exercises. Flora Belle's precocity exceeded music. Even at eleven, she knew how to give and receive pleasure. Before long she was completely enthralled by Helen Smithers.

"We're two of a kind," Helen had told her one sweet afternoon two years later as they lay naked in Helen's big bed. "You have come along better than any before. There'll never be another. I will be here for you always."

But, within the year they had parted. There had been others for Helen. Many others. Including every girl who had worked for Flora Belle in her sporting houses. None had refused, except golden, entrancing Rebecca Caldwell. The recollection brought a momentary flash of anger. Flora Belle regained her composure and smiled at Sue Ann. She found her fingers trembled with anticipation when she reached out toward the girl.

"Ah, you are doing nicely. What lovely little titties. Come closer, dear."

"I . . . ah, don't . . . think . . ."

"Don't let it worry you. There's no one else here. I'll be gentle with you, honestly I will. Come close. That's it. Closer to your dear Flora Belle. Aaah. So sweet. So very sweet." Flora Belle's fingers tingled when she stroked the satiny flesh of the trembling girl. Slowly she worked her hands downward, caressing the smooth, unblemished skin, sliding over the taut young belly. At last, she cupped the warm little mound and began to massage it skillfully.

"No," Sue Ann protested, a feeling of weakness spreading through her. "Please, don't . . . do . . . that . . ." Something seemed to explode inside her. She felt her will slipping away and made a desperate effort to stop it.

"Don't jerk away like that, Sue Ann, dear. I'm only being nice to you. Nicer than any man can be. What do they know of what a woman needs in love? Come here, let me teach you."

"Please, I don't want to do that," Sue Ann begged. "I don't want to."

Flora Belle felt a pang of remorse. Why was the child rejecting her offer of pleasure and satisfaction? Suddenly impatient, she reached out swiftly and grabbed Sue Ann by her slender arm.

"No!" Sue Ann yelled at her. In a blur, her free hand swung toward the frizzy-haired madam. The slap sounded loud in the luxurious bedroom.

A crimson splotch stained Flora Belle's left cheek. Anger rose, choking her. "Why you little bitch! I'll show you."

Before Flora Belle could react, Sue Ann wrenched

177

herself free and ran for the door that led to the sitting room, unmindful of her nakedness.

Rebecca's hand went to her hidden revolver at the sound of the slap. Then she realized that both the frightened girl and the woman were headed her way, both running on a collision course. She couldn't be caught here. Swiftly she turned and ran for her own room. Safely behind the door, she heard the entry to Flora Belle's suite bang open. She didn't hear the madam's furious hiss.

"I'll fix you good for this, you snotty bitch. I'm going to give you to Bobby O'Toole."

A few minutes later, though, Rebecca did hear Sue Ann's pitiful screams. The cries of pain changed to low moans, then resumed with greater intensity. Compelled by sympathy and anger, Rebecca threw her door open, determined to stop whatever torment the poor child was enduring.

Two of Ezekial's hardcase employees stood in the hallway. Their faces showed disgust, yet their hard eyes indicated their grudging willingness to follow orders.

"Everybody back in your rooms," one of them ordered. He took a threatening step toward Rebecca, his hand on his holstered Colt.

With the certain knowledge that she would never make it to her pistol in time, Rebecca retreated. Her spirit sank in regret and frustration. Only the belief in her own freedom kept her from despair.

In a few minutes the screams stopped.

Then Rebecca heard a familiar and hated voice bellowing in the hallway. "Man, that's the best I ever had. Boy, was she tight. And wriggle around . . . you've never seen the like."

Rebecca buried her face in her quaking hands. I will not give in, she promised herself. I will not cry. Not for me, not for Sue Ann. I will be strong and some day I will kill Bobby O'Toole.

Matt came back to her room by way of the saloon. He reached the door with a bottle of champagne tucked under one arm and glasses in hand. He rapped jauntily, aware of the baleful stare of the old swamper seated at the end of the hallway. Rebecca let him in.

"Where's the little girl?"

"She's dead, Matt," Rebecca said in a flat voice. She quickly told him of what had happened. "For that, as well as everything else, I'm going to kill O'Toole. Slowly and painfully."

"First we have to make sure of getting out of here."

"It should work like I told you. I'll get his attention, while you watch from here. When I have my gun on him, you join me. We'll put him out of the way and . . . just walk out the back."

"It's risky."

"I've learned a lot about the powers of a woman in a situation like this. I know it will work."

"What about your clothes?"

"I've lost my good beaded dress, my pistol and holster, moccasins, everything. I'll have to go in these." She made a deprecating gesture toward the saloon girl costume she wore.

"We'll get your things back."

Rebecca nodded approval and left the room. She walked swayingly, seductively toward the duffer who leaned against the wall in his tilted-back chair. He caught her motion from the corner of his eye and turned aged, but appreciative eyes on her. His expression told how much he liked her gait.

"I, ah, need some towels. A warm, wet one and some dry ones. My, ah, gentlemen caller had a messy accident."

"Went off in his pants, did he?" The old timer wheezed out a laugh at his own humor. His mirth ended when he looked into the muzzle of the Remington New Line in Rebecca's steady hand.

"If you say a word, I'll splatter your brains on that wall." She gestured to Matt, who hurried to join her. "Put him out," she ordered evenly.

From under his coat, Matt produced a long barreled Smith and Wesson No. 4 American, chambered for the .44 Russian cartridge. He smacked the heavy horse pistol along side the swamper's head. With a grunt and a soft sigh, the old man went slack in his chair. Matt extended the big pistol to Rebecca, butt first.

"Here, this is one of a pair. They were my father's. I want you to have them. They'll do a better job than that little Remington." He looked down at the unconscious man. "We'd better tie him up."

Rebecca removed her high heel shoes and net stockings. She handed the flimsy looking material to Matt. Soundlessly he twisted each of the stockings into a rope and used them to secure the swamper.

With the big No. 4 American in hand, Rebecca led the way down the back stairs. They neared the foot when light and sound spilled out of the saloon through a suddenly opened door. Rebecca and Matt froze.

"Thish . . . thish ain't the way to the outhouse," a slurred, drunken voice protested.

"It's the way out for you. You've had too much to drink," the burly barkeep growled.

Rebecca and Matt watched in anxious silence while the barman hustled the drunk to the back door and tossed him into the alley.

"I'm gonna complain to Mr. Caldwell about this," the expelled lush yelled to the shutting door.

The apron made it halfway back to the saloon when he looked up and saw Rebecca and Matt. His mouth dropped open and he started to yell. His eyeballs clicked left and right, in motion with the muzzle of the Smith American, which Rebecca waggled in a negative gesture.

"Up," she commanded in a whisper. The barkeep complied, raising his hands. "And don't make a sound. All three of us are going outside for a nice little chat." Rebecca swiftly descended the last few treads.

Directed by the steady pressure of the .44 in his back, the bartender led the way to the rear exit. He opened the latch and stepped out.

Once clear of the building, Rebecca raised the heavy barrel of the revolver and smashed it down on the man's head. He fell in a heap. The drunk looked up from the muddy alley.

"See? Tole you that you'd get yours." Then he passed out.

The two fleeing figures made two blocks without sighting anyone else. As they neared the livery corral, Tom Allison, the blacksmith, stepped out of the shadows and joined them. "All quiet," he said tersely.

Rebecca looked into the corral, seeking her own mount. An Indian pony nickered softly, his nostrils filled with the familiar scent of someone he knew. The animal worked through other nags to the rail nearest Rebecca.

"That's Lone Wolf's pony. He has to be here somewhere."

"Don't know what he looks like, but there's been nobody asking around about you. Are you sure it's his?"

"Yes, Matt, positive. If he's not been seen by

anyone, it's sure to mean he is in trouble. I can't be seen on the streets, which means you will have to do the looking. Please, it's important. I know something awful has happened."

SEVENTEEN

"What the hell do you mean, 'she's gone'?" a red-faced Ezekial Caldwell bellowed at Flora Belle Chase early the next morning. "Goddamnit, woman, you told me she was drugged, safe and tractable. Now you say she knocked out the towel boy and tied him up then did for the bartender, too. Why did you have to wait until now to let me know?"

Flora Belle felt the cold hand of fear tickling her spine. She had never seen Ezekial this angry before. "If you had been here, I would have told you earlier. The place was in an uproar. She had help, too. That sissy Peterson kid. Somehow he must have got her off the opium. Anyhow, it's done now. Not much I can do about it."

"Yes. And, oh, Christ, Jake's sure to find out. He'll chew nails. I . . . suppose I'd better be the one to tell him." Ezekial rose, his choleric face now ashen. God, Tulley would have his hide for this. To have Rebecca captive and not even tell Jake. His fat would be well fried before this day was over. And he had to do something about Flora Belle. That poor kid, Sue Ann. To let that monster, O'Toole have her because she wouldn't play bedroom games with Flora Belle, without even asking his permission, went too far.

"You acted stupidly last night. Not only in letting Rebecca escape, but in how you handled the little girl. What if she didn't want to play kissy-snatch with you?

183

That was no reason to give her to O'Toole. You knew how Bobby gets his jollies. It was a death warrant. *I* decide who goes and stays around here, not you, Flora Belle. Another couple of months and that Sue Ann would have been making us a fortune. You've cost me, and that means you've cost Bitter Creek Jake. I'm cutting your take by ten percent."

"What!" Flora Belle cried in wounded indignity. "I work hard to run a good place for you, you bastard. I earn my money."

"You acted like a fool and you're going to pay for it. From now on confine your bedroom gymnastics to those who appreciate them."

"She would have liked it. I know she would," Flora Belle responded in sullen defense. "She was just like me at that age . . . hot pants and eager to soothe the itch. She got scared, that's all."

"So you turned her over to a freak who blows his rocks watching little girls die. You're stupid, Flora Belle, stupid. I'm putting two men on the hallway from now on. No more of our girls are going to slip off in the night. Now, get out of my sight."

Matt Peterson walked the streets of Grub Stake deep in thought. Where could this Lone Wolf be? Rebecca had described him and Matt put out the word to the others who secretly worked to thwart Jake Tulley. So far he had received no results. Distracted, he crossed over to a sidestreet and began to walk in the direction of his former home. He passed the place with hardly a glance. Roger Styles had arrived, that much he knew. He also knew he hated the thought of anyone occupying the house that should be his. Seething with suppressed, impotent anger, he made another circuit of the town.

"Nothin', Matt. I'm sorry," Tom Allison told him at the blacksmithy. "I've asked around, but no one seems to know anything. She could be mistaken, you know."

"Not that gal," Matt defended Rebecca. "That Chase woman may have taken her memory away for a few days, but she's sharper than ever now." He smiled wistfully, recalling the previous night after they arrived at his shanty.

"Oh, it's so good to be here. Hold me, Matt," Rebecca had pleaded.

Their embrace quickly became one of passion. Matt felt the warmth of her body through his suit, his own ardor growing at the closeness of her. Their breathing became harsh and uneven. Matt slid one hand down her exquisite back to the narrow incurve above her firm, well-shaped bottom. She thrust herself against him eagerly and thrilled to the instant upsurge of his long penis. They kissed.

Rebecca's tongue sought his in the moist cavern of his mouth, playing tag and losing delightfully with each round. He reached his fullness and Rebecca stepped away from him.

Without speaking, she removed the saloon dress. Lamplight heightened the golden hue of her silky skin. To Matt her beauty was such as to make him ache with longing for her. His fingers fumbled like an inexperienced schoolboy while he removed his suit and shirt. The front of his underdrawers stood away from his body like a circus tent. Rebecca had recovered from her ordeal enough to be thrilled at the sight. This was what she wanted, needed, for oh, so long. She sank gratefully to her knees and drew the cotton cloth away from the object of her delight.

It swayed gracefully in the cool night air and she

took measure of it with both hands. Slowly she began to stroke him, taking pleasure from the satiny feel of the rigid flesh, watching the dark red tip pop out of sight, only to reappear, slick and glossy with eagerness. She leaned toward him.

"Oh, my dear, my dearest one," she murmured. Then her tongue began to inscribe spirals on the bulging head of his throbbing organ. He sank to his knees on a bear skin rug and drew her with him.

He reversed himself agilely and buried his face between her wide-spread thighs. He felt her shiver of delight as he neared his goal. His tongue flicked outward, tasting the sweet, heady nectar on the lacy folds of her outer chamber. She trembled at this delightful contact. Then it was his turn to shudder in ecstasy when she covered his burning manhood with cool, mobile lips.

Rebecca had a powerful mind of her own and determined to give as much pleasure as she received. No difficulty in that with this delightful man, she thought, her mind humming with happiness. Slowly she worked more of his massiveness into her mouth, deep down, questing for her inner secrets.

"Ceazin, Ceazin," she murmured in Sioux around his bountiful gift. All the way back here, the horror of her confinement receding, she had wanted it. Dreamed of this moment. Gratefully she took in more.

Suddenly her body rocked with new spasms as his tongue found her happy pebble, as the Oglala girls called it, and began to circle it rapidly, stimulating her to the brink, then withdrawing until she calmed for another assault. She had never reached fulfillment this way before and the prospect excited her further. Matt lapped at her eagerly, like a starving cat at a bowl of cream. Gradually she took in more of him, one hand holding the firm sack below his thick shaft, fingers gently kneading his balls.

New paroxysms of delight shook them both and their efforts redoubled. Then Matt found himself racing up the Olympian incline toward a thunderous climax. The girl beneath him writhed in the spell of her own approaching explosion and applied greater suction to his pulsating phallus, ingesting a bit more with each rhythmic tugging of her lips. Matt's tongue continued to slaver over the engorged nubbin at the top of her cleft, teasing, thrilling, bringing pleasure so great it nearly became agony.

At long last, though far too soon for either of them, they could hold back no longer. In a wild crescendo, they blazed out together. What an excruciatingly lovely experience. Over and over, Matt's tongue plumbed the depths of her pulsating channel, working deeper with each thrust. In her rhapsodic delight she continued to find and give satisfaction at both ends. Finally, they subsided.

Matt rolled off her and lay on his back against the soft fur of the bear, his head resting on that of the mounted animal. To Rebecca's delight, their powerful draining had not diminished his magnificent lance. She rose to her knees and straddled him, their eyes locked.

"Becky . . . oh, Becky, you're insatiable," he panted in mock protest.

"And so are you, my most darling man. Now, watch him. Watch him slide in his home. The perfect knife in the best fitting sheath." With torturous slowness, Rebecca impaled herself on Matt's huge shaft, sinking downward with an expression of utter contentment on her glowing face. It seemed hours until they had become fully joined.

Rebecca began to ride him. Matt watched, fascinated. The sight of his thick shaft, slick and glistening, plunging in and out of her rosy cleft excited him unbearably. Above him her breasts swayed in time with the energetic motion of her body. She tossed her head from side to side, transported on unending waves of joy. She used every muscle at her command to control and dominate, even while engaged in abject surrender. Suddenly her moment came upon her and she peaked in a frenzy. Then, almost at once, again. Now she increased her tempo, pulling Matt along with her until they cried out in mutual gratification.

With a start, Matt came back to the present. "No, she seems to be much better than ever," he reassured Tom. A small, nagging detail, which he had previously dismissed, returned to his consciousness. "I'm gonna take another look along the back streets. Over by way of my old place in particular. See you around, Tom."

He walked past the mansion again, eyes carefully scanning every detail. What had it been that had fixed in his mind before? What . . . or who? That was it. A gunhawk stood out by the coal shed, a Winchester cradled in his folded arms. Why would anyone put a guard on a coal shed? Suddenly Matt had the answer.

He knew where to find Lone Wolf.

"Are you out of your mind, Zeke?" Jake Tulley shouted at his second in command. "I thought you had brains. Personal revenge my ass! You had that murdering bitch right here in town, turnin' tricks in your whorehouse, and you never once thought to tell me? Why, Zeke, why? You could have made a lot of money by turnin' her over to me. Now we're gonna

188

have to find her before she causes more trouble."

"I wouldn't mind spreading her legs again," Roger Styles said wistfully from the corner of the room. He peered at the inch of rich, amber brandy in the large balloon glass he held negligently in his left hand. "She fought like a wildcat."

"Hell, you raped her," Ezekial accused.

"True, Ezekial. You know how the old saying goes, 'Any sissy can have seduction, but a he-man wants his rape.' This really is an annoyance, Ezekial. Had you done properly, she would be dead now and there would be no one to put a possible rock in our path. I must agree with Jake on this. Let me see, what should we do to discipline you for this breach of trust?"

"Take a cut of his loot?" Jake suggested greedily.

"No. Something more original than that. What say we cut off his balls?"

Ezekial's face paled and he sagged at the knees.

"Only joking, old boy," Roger continued. "Actually, though, you should have an object lesson. I'd suggest giving control of the Mother Lode to Flora Belle, but she's directly responsible for Rebecca's escape." Roger's voice grew hard and cold. "I want that girl found and brought here. I want her dead, dead, dead. Do I make myself clear? You, Ezekial will make it your top priority. Find your niece and bring her to me. If I don't get her head . . . yours will do."

Ezekial swallowed around the lump of fear in his throat. "Yes, Mr. Styles. Yes, sir."

Slim Malone hated guard duty. He had deserted from the Ninth New York during the Civil War because of the hours of post walking he had been compelled to do. It was boring. Especially at night. Slim stifled a yawn and walked around the side of the shack to relieve himself. He rested his Winchester against the coal shed and undid his fly. He extracted his penis and began to release a stream of urine. Piss on all watch details, he thought.

The knife came hissing out of the darkness.

It buried to the hilt, low in Slim's abdomen. He gripped convulsively at his flaccid penis and dropped to his knees in his own waste. His mouth worked in a futile effort to bring forth the agonized scream that clawed at the inside of his chest. He didn't hear stealthy footsteps approach him from the back of the lot, nor did his eyes—squeezed shut in pain—see the figure of a broad-shouldered miner. The muscular drill hand raised a short-handled maul and smashed its heavy head down on Slim's skull. A moment's brightness preceded an eternity of darkness and death.

Soundlessly, three dark shapes joined the single-jack operator. They grouped around the padlocked door. The miner lifted the large lock case in hard, callused fingers. "Damn, that looks like a mighty good lock. Take forever to file it off."

"Let me see it, Cal," Matt Peterson whispered. He studied the object for a moment, then groped in a trouser pocket. He came out with a large ring of keys. "My father's," he explained. "He had a duplicate set of every lock in the house and at the saloon. One of these ought to fit." Matt tried several without results. Then he inserted a hollow brass tube with a snake's back crook attached to it. Slowly he twisted. The hasp snapped open.

"There," the young man announced proudly.

Rebecca Caldwell pressed inside ahead of him. In the darkness she saw little, though she sensed the presence of someone. She struck a Lucifer match and shielded its glow with her cupped hands. Immediately her eyes widened in surprise and anger.

Lone Wolf sagged against his chains, suspended by his arms, unable to sit or any longer to stand upright. A cruel iron collar surrounded his neck and the links from its back led to the rafters. He was filth-begrimed from the remainder of last winter's coal and blood-crusted welts stood out on his face. He raised his head warily, expecting another beating.

"You took long enough to get here," he croaked. A slow smile of relief blossomed on his face.

A pained expression broke through the relief of finding her companion alive. Rebecca knew what he must feel to be tethered like a rabid beast. The unequaled and unfettered freedom of the plains Indians gave a man a sort of greatness. The horror of bondage diminished him . . . in his eyes and in those in his peers. New resolve for vengeance glowed in Rebecca's eyes.

"Are . . . these . . ." She pointed to the bindings. "Did these belong to your father?"

"No. I've never seen them before."

"We'll have to rip them out of the wall then, with no key."

"That'll make a lot of noise," Matt cautioned.

"We have to take that chance. Otherwise we have come for nothing. Try to find something to pry with."

Matt came up with a spike-ended bar. He handed it to Cal and the powerful miner jammed it under a large, turned over nail. He heaved mightily and the softer metal gave. It opened out and one chain fell free. On the other sidewall, he discovered the link had been fastened with a huge staple. It took all his effort to wedge the least part of the tip under and wiggle the bar. The 'U' shaped fastener didn't budge.

Cal slammed the bar into the junction of chain and staple and managed to drive a bit more tip under this time. He put all the strength of his thick shoulders against the iron rod and pulled it toward him. Wood squeaked in protest and then the purchase slipped.

"Damn!" he swore under his breath. He made ready to try again.

"Hold it," Rebecca cautioned. "You'd better undo the one in the ceiling first. Otherwise you'll hang him."

Cal looked sheepish. "Sorry, Ma'am." He moved closer to Lone Wolf and studied the fastening. Some sort of shackle and bolt arrangement. And them without any wrenches. He reached up and tested the rafter. It gave springily.

Cal applied all his strength and body weight. The rafter bowed downward, its ends shrieking against the nails. Then, with a crack like a .22 pistol shot, it broke near the center. Lone Wolf's neck chain fell clear. Once more, Cal went back to the stubborn staple.

Two more attempts ended in success. With a squeak of metal against wood and rattle of metallic links, the chain dropped away. Lone Wolf staggered to a wall and leaned against it.

"That you in there, Slim?" a voice called from outside.

Everyone froze. Then Matt replied in a muffled voice. "Yeah. Who did you think it would be?"

"Well, what the hell are you doin'? You know no one is supposed to go around the prisoner."

"He wanted a drink of water," Matt replied for the dead Slim.

"Ain't you the regular nurse now." The door opened and the speaker walked in, directly into the fat muzzle of the .44 American in Rebecca's hands. The idea of giving the alarm under such circumstances never entered his head. He gaped, slack-jawed, and took in the faces before him. He'd remember them. He would never take his eyes off them until they left and he could call for help.

Wrong, he found out when Cal slugged him with the hefty single-jack mallet.

The two dead men were found at the four o'clock guard change. Immediately Jake Tulley roused the rest of his gang, there and at the Mother Lode. First Rebecca made good her escape, now they had lost their prisoner. When the men assembled in the side yard of the Peterson mansion, he gave them quick, explicit orders.

"Search every house, store and shed in this town. Block all roads out and don't let anyone leave. I want that damned half-breed bitch and the white Injun's ridin' with her. Turn everything upside down until you find them."

"People ain't gonna like that," Long Tom Wheeler observed.

"Fuck 'em. Do it anyway."

While the destructive, totally illegal search of Grub Stake went on, Rebecca, Lone Wolf and Matt met with the cadre of resistance fighters they had summoned to Doc Silver's house half a mile from town.

"The time has come to act," Rebecca told the assembled miners, Kathlene O'Day and banker Ross. "Lone Wolf has been held prisoner, so was I. He came back from Denver to say we can expect no help from the U.S. marshal. At least not in time to do any good. Tulley and his men will get frantic now, they will go to any lengths to find us and destroy your opposition. If we move fast, not give them the chance to organize against us, we have a chance. There will be no better time later. We have to clean house on the whole gang now."

"We're with you on that, Miss Rebecca," Ross replied for the rest.

"Aye and that's the truth of it," Kathlene O'Day got in.

"What do we need to do?"

"Talk to everyone you have sounded out about fighting. Get all the arms and ammunition you can and be ready when the shooting starts. Also, it would help to have as much dynamite available as possible. These boys are gunslingers, some of them top names. But a Colt don't stand up so well against a stick of Hercules."

Little Rubin Silver clattered into the room, back from his scouting mission toward town. The ten year old was breathless, his black hair tousled and his eyes wide. "There are roadblocks on all ways out of town," he reported. "An' those awful *mensch* are searching everybody's house. People are sure mad about it."

"That should work to our advantage," Rebecca observed. "Everyone leave now, talk to all the people you can. We will attack at first light."

EIGHTEEN

"You ain't gonna stop me this time," Hard Rock Mike told the people remaining in Doc Silver's kitchen. "This is workin' up to be a good fight and I'm gonna be in it."

"You are in no condition to be running around the streets shooting it out with outlaws," the doctor protested.

"I could sit down and shoot, couldn't I?"

"Ah . . . yes," Doc Silver hesitated. "Only where?"

"How many two story buildings are there in town?" Mike inquired, enjoying himself.

"The Mother Lode and the bank," Brian Ross replied.

"Then, if you'll trust me in the upstairs of your bank, I can potshoot all of the main street from a window."

"He has a point," Rebecca directed toward the doctor. "And we can use every man we can get."

"Then it's settled," Mike concluded in a satisfied tone. He spoke next to Rebecca. "If you folks can rig some way to get me from here to there, I'd be obliged. And . . . I want to pick up a little something on the way."

Dawn still lingered some fifteen minutes away. All of the houses in Grub Stake had been searched, as had every business except the bank. Most of Tulley's men were drinking coffee or beer at the Mother Lode. Those on roadblock duty grumbled over their fate.

"We're supposed to be here to keep that white squaw and her wild man friend from gettin' outta town, right? Well, if they didn't find any sign of them *in* town, how can they be tryin' to get *out?*"

That makes sense, Pete," the complainer's companion remarked. "But we just gotta look at it like this was an army . . . or a sort of police department. With them, there's always some stupid thing a feller's expected to do. With the pay we're gettin', I'm not gonna complain too much. Though I could sure stand a cup of coffee."

"I'm for that," Pete enthused. "Hey, you keep a watch and I'll go get us some."

"Fine with me."

Pete made it half a block down the street when he heard horses' hoofs approaching behind him, from out of town. Well, there'd been a few people come in during the search. Their orders were to keep people from getting out, not in. He ignored it and took another step. Then a pistol shot ripped open the pre-dawn quiet. Pete whirled and saw five persons bearing down on him, six-guns out, horses at a full gallop. Beyond them he saw the body of his buddy sprawled in the dust.

"Gaw-damn!" the runty highwayman exclaimed, one hand clawing for his Colt.

One of the riders, it was a girl Pete had time to see, leveled a big revolver at him and he watched it spout fire and buck in her hand. The next instant, he felt an enormous pain in his chest and some unseen force picked him off his feet. He slammed into a tie-rail and rolled to one side. The blackness of the void replaced false dawn for Pete.

Rebecca and those with her rode past the corpse-draped hitching rail and angled sharply across the street to the bank. Brian Ross and Hard Rock Mike dismounted and ran to the door. The banker produced a key and let Mike in. Then he returned to his mount.

By then, several of Tulley's hardcases had poured into the street from the Mother Lode. They looked toward the intruders, only to break apart in confusion when gunshots sounded from several points around town. Instantly the riders whirled their horses and charged the indecisive outlaws.

"Shoot to kill," Rebecca shouted over the din of battle. "We haven't time or a way to take prisoners." She illustrated her order with another blast from her No. 4 Smith.

To Rebecca's right, Lone Wolf's big Sharps belched flame and an ear-ringing roar. Down the block, one of Tulley's hardcases bent double and fell over the railing of the balcony fronting the Mother Lode. Lone Wolf reloaded.

"Let's clear them off the street," Rebecca decided. She kicked heels into her mount's flanks and reined him to the right. In the lead, six-gun blasting a path through the rank of outlaws, Rebecca galloped along Main Street, Lone Wolf, Brian Ross and Tom Allison in her wake.

Gunmen scattered and sought refuge from the whirlwind of lead that chipped wood from building fronts, geysered dust from the roadway and bit into their vulnerable flesh. The grim-faced, determined riders who thundered toward the assortment of highwaymen and grifters looked like the Four Horsemen to them and they quickly melted away to safer environs. Three of them remained behind, in spreading pools of their own blood. Horses flashed past, Rebecca still in the lead, and closed on the front of the Mother Lode.

Two gunhawks jumped apart, then tried to reach the batwing doors at the same time. They succeeded a second before a .44 slug from Rebecca's No. 4 smacked into the back of one outlaw. He remained draped across the swinging door while his companion vanished inside, hurried by the lead that buzzed around his head. The riders swung left and headed toward the far end of town.

"Dang it, Matt, them fellers can keep us here all day," a wizened miner in his mid-fifties complained. "I can pick 'em off easily with m'squirrel rifle, but they keep sendin' more boys up to that roadblock."

"I've been studying on it, Lou," Matt Peterson told him. "We have to break through there. Get another man, rig a couple of sticks of dynamite, real short fuses. Then work your way to where you can throw them behind those overturned wagons. When it goes off, the rest of us will charge."

Lou produced a toothless grin. "Them's sweet words, Matt. Reminds me of the time at Manassas Junction. I was with Bobby Lee's boys. We ran them Yankees over with artil'ry, powder, shot and bayonets. I'll get Zeb Taylor. He's a good hand at throwin' things."

After Lou left, Matt had some second thoughts. He had never been a soldier, had no experience at command. What if he led these brave men to their deaths? He gnawed on his lower lip a moment, then heard a flurry of shots from the center of town. His indecision was holding up their only chance to get rid of Tulley and his hoodlums. When Lou signaled the ready, Matt hurried among the other miners, to tell them of the charge he planned to make.

Behind the improvised barricade, the gunhawks peered over at the once timid men who now stormed them with deadly determination. Slowly the firing dwindled from both sides. Lem Carter stood and called to the miners.

"You out there. Throw down your guns. You can't whup us. They's too many of us. We're here to help you, to bring law and order. Do as I say, now, ya hear?"

Lou's dynamite stick landed at Lem Carter's feet. It blew him into three ugly, ragged chunks.

"Let's go, men!" Matt Peterson shouted. "Charge!"

The second dynamite blast went off. Another tower of dust rose and obscured the scene, while the miners, teamsters and townspeople ran forward, firing from the hip. In the lead, Matt Peterson raised his father's other No. 4 American and blasted the face off a scraggly bearded badman, switched targets and downed an outlaw who had all the fighting he wanted and attempted to run from the battle. He jolted forward, off his feet and into a mud puddle.

Quickly the attackers swarmed over the defenses and fell upon the last of the gunmen. A sudden rattle of gunfire from up the street brought Matt's head around. Rebecca and three men galloped down on the last surviving gunslingers, weapons blazing. In a moment the struggle ended. Not a member of the gang survived.

"You got here just in time," Matt told Rebecca through a relieved grin.

"We aim to please."

"You aim pretty well, too."

Some of the gang managed to reach the livery corral through back alleys, dodging bullets on the way. Hastily they rounded up jittery horses, threw on saddles and rode out of the slide-pole gate.

"Which way?" one of the newcomers demanded.

"Through town and out the other way," Clyde Morton suggested. "We'll take as many of those sons of bitches as we can."

More of the assaulting force had concentrated on

Main Street now, throwing many, often poorly aimed, shots at the outlaws. With pistols blazing, the escaping owlhoots leaped their mounts into rapid motion. Shoulders churning, the horses ripped clots of dirt from the street as they raced toward the guns of the miners and townsmen. Two hardcases flew from the saddle, a third groaned and slumped forward. On they charged.

Then, as they neared the bank, the ground around them erupted in multiple blasts like an artillery barrage. Horses reared, whinnying in fright, men fell from their backs. Others forced their way onward.

Mike Hoxsey sat in the window above them, a stick of dynamite between each finger of his right hand. He lit the fuses with a stubby cigar and flipped the deadly cylinders out as the survivors broke free of the dust and flying debris of the first explosions. Loud blasts sounded and more horses and men went down, shrieking in agony. Laughing in fiendish glee, Mike picked up his Winchester, levered a round into the chamber and cut down on a survivor attempting to crawl away to the safety of a filled water trough.

Inside the Silver Creek Cafe, Kathlene O'Day watched the outlaws ride down on the town's defenders. A variety of weapons barked loudly, while dust and powder smoke lay in a thick haze over everything. Then, suddenly, loud blasts sounded and the street erupted in gouts of dirt, mangled flesh and flying bits of wood and metal. One of the big windows bowed inward and disintegrated in a shower of glass.

"Holy St. Patrick," she gasped aloud. "Sure an' the devil's gonna have a busy day today."

Three new blasts rent the air and, in their wake, she heard the tinkle of more breaking windows. Out of the maelstrom rushed three bedraggled outlaws, two of them bleeding from the ears and nose. They headed directly toward the door of the Silver Creek. Another hardcase crawled toward a water trough two doors down.

A rifle cracked from the upstairs of the bank across the street and the creeping man stiffened with the impact of a bullet. He sprawled in the dirt and his legs kicked out a tattoo of death. Kathlene turned her attention back to the trio that approached her cafe. They hit the boardwalk and the center man raised his leg for a powerful kick.

The door flew open and the fleeing bandits crowded into the narrow space.

Two of them flew back out into the street, propelled by a blast of buckshot pellets from the Parker shotgun in Kathlene's hands. The third, although hampered by two lead balls in his left shoulder, advanced on her, an evil leer on his face.

He quickly learned his mistake. The second barrel of Kathlene's Parker discharged and, through the curling smoke, she saw the gunslinger flung back against the doorpost, his belly a bleeding mass of mangled flesh.

"Faith and the lad'll be standin' before Satan before his husk drops to the floor." Kathlene wiped the sweat from her brow with the back of one hand, patted a stray wisp of hair into her tightly-drawn bun and reloaded the shotgun.

Few of the newly recruited gunmen had a taste for this sort of battle. Why stay around for the lynch party that these angry citizens would probably throw after they finished shooting up the place, they reasoned. Despite shouted commands from Tulley's loyal crew, they took to their heels. Quickly they rounded up horses, under fire constantly, and rode out the opposite direction from where the fighting raged. They paid no attention to Clyde Morton, who crawled through the shattered ruin of horses and men on the main drag and disappeared into an alley. He made slow, cautious progress to the far end, checked the street carefully, then made a dash toward the front of the mansion. Animal cunning told him he would be safer near the big boss.

Inside, Roger Styles hastily packed a large pair of saddle bags. How in hell could such a thing be happening? What incredible bungling. Ezekial has the girl, then he doesn't and now the whole grand plan was falling down around him. He glanced nervously at the window.

Outside, on the broad front lawn, seven gunmen stood guard to prevent the attackers from reaching the inside of the mansion. While Roger watched, the surly young punk, Clyde Morton, joined the others. With misfits like that, it's no wonder Tulley's men could not stand off a mob of amateurs. One of the gunhawks shouted and pointed down the street.

A dozen miners and mill workers rounded the corner and advanced on the mansion, those in the lead appeared to be dragging a large brass nozzle. A hose was attached to it. Was there a fire? The possibility added to Roger's discomfort. Below, the gang members raised their weapons.

Suddenly a white billow burst from the hose. A hissing roar followed it down the street. Live steam, Roger thought and his stomach wrenched at the prospect of its fiery breath touching his flesh. The men Tulley had sent to protect him didn't fare too well, he observed from behind the safety of the window glass.

The scalding vapor reached the men on the lawn. It seared flesh and clawed at throats. Five outlaws fell, writhing and screaming, on the sparse grass. Others tried to run. Gunshots erupted from the attacking

202

miners. Two men fell. The last one shrieked and reeled off, his flesh bright pink. Here and there some survivors had open, running sores where the skin had burst. Frightened for his life, Roger turned away.

"John!" he yelled down the stairwell. "Trapper John! Get up here at once." Instant, reassuring footsteps comforted him.

Clyde Morton ached. He hurt in every part of his body. They had cooked him! Those bastard miners had cooked him alive with steam. His face felt swollen and he could hardly see out of his eyes. He shakily brought up a hand and looked at the skin. Bright red. A groan escaped from his mouth. From behind him, in the house, he heard a rapid rattle of shots. The miners retreated with their infernal device. Clyde began to crawl on his hands and knees.

He had no idea of where he was going, only that he wanted to be far from here. They would come back, he felt sure of that. Ahead, to his left, he saw the entrance to the alley through which he had recently run. Fearful of pursuit, he crawled that way, wincing at the pain each movement caused. Fifty feet to go, he thought. Twenty . . . ten . . . He collapsed momentarily in the safety of the enclosed passageway.

Rested, he tried to stand. The torment of his scalded flesh shrieked through his savaged nerves. He could not bear his weight upright. Morton dropped to his knees and continued to crawl through the alley. Ahead lay Main Street. Would his prospects be any better?

The main battlefield came into Morton's view. To his left was the bank. With the dynamite throwing sniper there, he had no desire to head that direction. The other way . . . led to the road out of town. He turned his head that direction, skin crying out in protest, and saw the form of a man standing with his back to the alley. The figure looked familiar.

Then Morton had it. Peterson, that mealy-mouthed sissy, Matt Peterson. He and the wild Indian girl who escaped from the Mother Lode were behind this all. He could hardly stand the agony of drawing his Colt. Hatred fired his eyes and the bubbling fury in his veins overcame the misery of his body. Slowly Clyde Morton slid the blued-steel revolver out of its holster and forced his chattering nerves under control, willing his arm to move faster before his enemy got away.

The Colt came into Clyde's view, the blade front sight lining up on Matt Peterson's back. It took both of Clyde's thumbs to cock the hammer. He licked dry, tender lips and began to squeeze the trigger.

Rebecca stood facing Matt. "From the sound of it, the fightin's almost over. Now's the time to go after Tulley and Roger Styles. I want to settle with Bobby O'Toole and *dear* Uncle Ezekial, too."

"We'll try the Mother Lode first," Matt suggested.

As he spoke, Rebecca heard the ratcheting of a Colt's hammer. She started to look about for the source of the threatening sound when it blasted through the early morning air. Matt seemed to leap toward her, eyes wide in shock, arms flying wildly at his sides. He half turned on one heel and toppled to the ground. A large hole showed clearly in the dark cloth of his suit coat, on the right side, near the center of his back.

"Matt!" Rebecca cried out. "Oh, my God, Matt!"

She sank to her knees at his side, while grief and guilt tore at her soul. It was her fault. If she hadn't let him get mixed up in all this, he would still be alive and unhurt. He would still be alive! Anguish shredded her. Oh, how she loved him. Kind, gentle, a lover beyond any expectations, now lying in the dirt, bleeding his life away. Her hand darted out and felt the area of the wound. Under the shoulder blade. Good. He might . . . maybe have a chance. Once more the metallic clicks of a Colt hammer brought her attention back to the present.

Her sensitive ears identified the direction without doubt. She brought her head up and looked into the raving eyes of Clyde Morton, the muzzle of his six-gun pointed unwaveringly in her direction. Rebecca's right hand moved only slightly.

Her Smith & Wesson No. 4 spoke with violent authority.

Clyde Morton seemed to spring into the air, still spread-eagled, then he dropped back on the dusty street. The heavy .44 slug had struck him in the area of his right collar bone. His Colt had fired harmlessly into the air then flew from his useless hand. Even before he struck the ground, his left hand clawed frantically for the pistol. His fingers brushed the hot metal of the barrel and hope flared in him.

It died when Rebecca's .44 roared again. The bullet slammed into the top of Clyde Morton's head and exploded his brains out his ears.

At Rebecca's feet, Matt moaned and she turned her attention to him. She saw motion on the other side of her and glanced up to see Doc Silver kneeling in the dust. Quickly and competently the doctor examined Matt, then turned a smile toward Rebecca.

"It is an extremely serious wound. The bullet most surely pierced the lung. But, in a man young and strong like Matt, it isn't necessarily fatal. I'll do what I can now. You go on and do what you must. I came to tend the wounded."

"Th-thank you, doctor." Rebecca rose and carefully reloaded her .44. Lone Wolf rode up and dismounted.

"Nearly all of Tulley's men have been killed or they

ran off," he told her.

"I gathered that. We have to go after Tulley and Roger."

Lone Wolf glanced down at Matt. "Is he . . . ?"

"No. Doctor Silver says he has a chance to live. He's one more I'm going to make them pay for." Together they started for the Mother Lode.

A block down the street, a sudden flurry of shots pinned them down. Lone Wolf ducked behind a flour barrel at the mercantile, while Rebecca flattened herself behind the dubious cover of an overturned pine-plank bench. Both hunters looked about for their hidden enemy.

"Over there," Rebecca whispered to Lone Wolf. "In that doorway to the old dancehall. I think it's Rupe Denton."

"I see him. And down there toward the corner. Bobby O'Toole."

"I want that fat bastard for myself," Rebecca hissed.

"You've got him. Give me some covering fire and I'll try to flank them through the back streets."

Rebecca and Lone Wolf opened up at once. The white warrior came to his feet and ran back the direction they had come from, ducked into the alley, leaped Clyde's corpse and hurried along toward the back street.

Denton lay sprawled in the recessed entrance to the dancehall. He sighted under a wagon standing at the side of the street and put a shot into the bench that sheltered Rebecca. The heavy wood leaped back toward her face and splinters flew. The spent slug smacked into an adobe wall. Rebecca returned fire. Denton sent two more rounds her way.

Rebecca studied the situation. The angle was bad and she could not get a clear view of her opponent. She eased herself along behind the bench. Hummm, from here, she considered. Carefully she took aim and fired at the curved iron tire of the rear wagon wheel.

Lead howled off strap iron and altered course so that it slammed into the opening where Denton lay. By chance, it gouged flesh from the back of his left shoulder. Pain and reflex forced Denton to move before reason could prevent it. He came into Rebecca's view for only a second.

It was long enough.

Two slugs sped from the .44 caliber No. 4 and smacked into Rupe Denton's chest. He flew backward and struck the barred door of the dancehall. Blood poured from the large, irregular exit wounds. He slid to the plank entry way and remained in a sitting position. An expression of utter disbelief froze on his face. No slip of a li'l gal could do that to him.

He carried that conviction with him into hell.

Quickly Rebecca snapped open her Smith and replaced the spent cartridges. Not many left, she observed. Out of the corner of her eye, she saw sudden motion down the street.

Bobby O'Toole moved fast for a fat man. His three hundred pounds of lard and muscle jiggled as his thick-thighed legs churned under him. He had only four rounds left. To face that hellion? he asked himself in fear. No way. He had to get away, find more ammunition. Although he would never admit it aloud to his peers, Bobby O'Toole was terrified of Rebecca. Her determination to get revenge on him and all of Jake Tulley's gang struck him numb with fear. Worst of all, he had visions of being taken alive and facing the black-hooded hangman. Of all possible fates, the thought of a noose around his neck turned Bobby's insides to jelly. A glance over his shoulder showed him Rebecca coming after him, six-gun at the ready. He fired a hasty shot that missed.

NINETEEN

The instant the bullet left his muzzle, Bobby O'Toole ducked behind a filled water barrel to one side of the barbershop. Rebecca's return shot punched a hole in the wooden container. A thin stream arched out, the contents spilling on the plankwalk. Aware that his flimsy protection now trickled away from him, O'Toole shuffled along the walkway, bent low, away from the threat of Rebecca's Smith & Wesson.

Fear-sweat emanated from his armpits as he fled. He had only five rounds left. The moment he came into view, Rebecca fired again. The .44 bullet threw Bobby up against the wall of an abandoned building, the hot lead cutting a deep groove in his cartridge belt. He stumbled and nearly fell, regained balance and ran wildly away from her.

Implacably, Rebecca followed. Ahead she saw an ore hopper and anticipated O'Toole's tactics. The moment before he turned to duck behind it, she fired. The slug split wood from a roof support and howled off along the street. Bobby O'Toole raised up slightly, the barrel of his Remington resting on the top of the ore hopper. He eared back the hammer and took aim. In the same instant he squeezed the trigger, Rebecca moved forward and to the left.

The bullet moaned past her right ear. The distance between them had closed to less than twenty yards.

Again O'Toole loosed a round. It, too, missed the

intended target. Rebecca took a step out toward the center of the street.

Her mind worked quickly and clearly. She judged the angle of the metal funnel at the top of the hopper-crusher implement. From here, she gauged, she might be able to make another ricochet shot. She brought up the heavy No. 4 American and took careful aim.

A forty-four round struck the iron frame and howled off toward the overhang above. A miss.

Close enough, though, that Bobby O'Toole lost his nerve. He scrambled away on hands and knees, then lurched to his feet and ran toward the dark rectangle of shadow that indicated an alley mouth. He directed his body to deliver more speed and glanced fearfully over his shoulder. His eyes bulged at what he saw.

A big black hole. Rebecca held the .44 Smith in both hands, legs wide-spread, the sight initially on the back of O'Toole's head. At the last instant she reminded herself she wanted his death to be long and painful. She lowered the front blade and realigned on his leg. The No. 4 roared.

Bobby O'Toole spun to his right and hurtled to the ground. He struck chin first. His protruding belly saved him from a broken neck. Fright overriding the pain, he scrabbled with clawing fingers and boot toes in an effort to reach the alley. To his jangled mind it seemed he hardly moved, though he covered ground at a respectable pace. In only seconds he placed the thick protection of a wall between him and the vengeance-minded girl. Before he thought, he threw a hasty shot behind in her direction.

Relentlessly Rebecca came after him.

O'Toole hauled himself down the alleyway. Behind him he heard her taunting voice.

"I'm saving you, O'Toole. I won't kill you. You're going to hang. Right here in Grub Stake. We'll take a big coil of rope and make a noose, then string you up to the old pine at the edge of town."

Oh, nooo! his mind wailed in terror-struck silence. Not a hanging. Ahead he saw the indentation of a side door. He quickly reached it and squeezed his bulk into the depression, waiting. He heard Rebecca's footsteps enter the alley. He licked dry, trembling lips and counted to four. Then he swung his head and arm out and fired a hurried shot.

The slug missed and Rebecca brought up the No. 4. She eared back the single action hammer and squeezed off. The hammer fell on a spent cartridge.

Grinning hysterically, Bobby O'Toole cocked his revolver and took slow, deliberate aim. His hammer, too, fell on a dead casing. Horror washed over his face and he hurtled himself out of the doorway. Painfully he limped and dragged himself along until he found himself caught in the inside angle of the 'L' shaped alleyway. To his right, at the far end of the long leg of the L he saw Lone Wolf approaching. In the other direction, Rebecca had holstered her empty revolver and drawn a wicked, curved-bladed skinning knife. Grimly she advanced on him.

Bobby O'Toole drew his own large, fighting Bowie and watched Rebecca come toward him with the fascination a bird has for a deadly snake. Her words echoed hotly in his brain. Oh, God, not a hanging. Unconsciously his left hand went to his throat and he massaged the purplish scar hidden beneath the neckerchief . . .

. . ."There he goes!" angry voices howled from the narrow main street of the small Kansas town. "Get that monster."

Bobby O'Toole ran in stark terror. Why did they want to hurt him? He'd not done anything to make them so mad. Why, she . . . she'd even said she liked to have someone touch her there. She'd eagerly hauled down her little bloomers and let him run his trembling fingers over her chubby, hairless mound. He'd pulled off his own clothes and then hers and she leaned forward and licked his hairy chest when he thrust a thick finger into her juicy tunnel. She'd wriggled on the hay and giggled when he positioned her and knelt between her legs. His short, thick penis ached for release by the time he pressed it against her hot, moist cleft.

It opened slightly and he entered a short way. Her eyes went wide with the pain, though she didn't cry out. He forced himself a little harder and shivered as the exciting tightness yielded. He didn't feel any tearing release and knew that someone had been here before him. That didn't bother him. It was better sometimes not to plow a muddy field. Bobby raised himself on his elbows and began to sway his hips back and forth. She put her arms around his neck and her little legs stuck into the air at a wide angle, too short to lock around his waist. She giggled and cooed and it took a long time before Bobby felt the tension rising and his body throbbed for release. Then he did it. Like always. The best part.

His big Bowie slashed across her throat. Her dying spasms and the magnificent contractions of the muscles around her slippery passage brought him to an explosive discharge, drained all his sap and left him weak and shaken. Slowly, reluctantly, he withdrew his still rigid shaft.

"You was good, honey. Real good," he whispered to her.

He found a bucket of water, washed off and dressed. He left the big barn on the small Kansas farm. He felt certain he would be miles away before her father came looking for the girl.

His belief proved wrong. He had stopped in the small town of Gage for a beer and a plate of the free lunch. A wagon clattered into town and before it stopped the occupant howled out his grief and horror. His little daughter raped and murdered. The body was in the back. Bobby O'Toole blanched and headed for the back door of the saloon.

The manhunt was on.

It ended a few minutes later when Bobby rounded a corner and walked into ten rifle and shotgun toting citizens. They wasted little time. They pressed the farmer's wagon into service. Bobby was tied hand and foot. The murdered girl's father personally tied the hangman's knot. A raging crowd, the scene illuminated by flaming torches, dragged him to the edge of town. The grieving, but furious father slung the rope over the thick limb of a cottonwood and fitted the noose. Bobby's legs gave way, he wet himself and cowered in terror on the bed of the wagon box. He could still smell the scent of the girl's blood, drained on the wooden bed beside him.

"Oh, noooo! Oh, God, please don't," he begged them. "I didn't do nothin'! She teased me, begged me to do it, dared me. I . . . I didn't hurt her. I didn't!"

Three muscle-bulging Kansas farm hands stood him up. The town marshal lashed the mules and they jerked the wagon out from under him. The rope bit cruelly into his flesh and the world went black. Then salvation came.

Riding hard, the rest of the gang Bobby rode with at the time thundered down on the site of his execution. Their flurry of bullets drove the townspeople and farmers away. With a swift knife slash, the boss of the gang cut the rope above Bobby's neck and dumped the fat killer over his saddle. They rode out in another fusillade of pistol shots, leaving behind five dead citizens.

The boss had given him hell, sure. But at least he was alive. Oh, God, he prayed he would never see a rope again . . .

. . . ."I'm going to watch you hang," Rebecca repeated.

Bobby O'Toole's mind reeled and he saw Rebecca as she looked on the day nearly six years ago. The day when Jake Tulley had traded her and her mother to Iron Calf for the lives of the surviving gang members. Nice little body, big tits and a swell ass. A little old for him, though he wouldn't have minded taking her down on the creek bank for a little fun. Now she wanted to hang him. His insides trembled, his knees refused to support him and, as on that night long ago in Kansas, his bladder let go, flooding his legs with a hot, wet stream. He blinked and the present day Rebecca came into focus again, three paces closer. The keen edge of the knife in her hand glinted in the morning light. Reflexively, he flicked out with the Bowie, fear stink hovering around his fat body.

Rebecca ignored the premature slash and stepped even closer. A beatific smile suddenly lighted her lips. Her eyes had a distant gaze, as though seeing a longed for lover. She came within arm's reach of Bobby O'Toole.

He stared at her face, transfixed.

"Let me shoot him," Lone Wolf offered.

"No. This will do. I have him exactly where I want him," Rebecca replied. "Now, fat pig, do you remember the day you and Tulley and those scum uncles of mine gave us to the Sioux?"

"Nunnn . . . aaaah, yes. Yes I do. I . . . I didn't really want to, you know. Honest, I was against it. You was . . . too pretty for that."

"I'm sure you felt that way. Had something nice all figured out for me yourself, eh?" Her Oglala skinning knife flicked out.

Bobby O'Toole felt a searing line of agony cross his fat belly. His shirt lost its usual tightness and he looked down to see blood running in a sheet down the pallid flesh of his lower abdomen. His eyes went round and rolled up and he screamed.

Again Rebecca's knife whispered through the air and another searing trail of torment slid across his bulging gut. This time Rebecca used far greater wrist pressure. The blade disappeared into the layers of lard and muscle and with delicate precision split the peritoneal sack.

Bobby O'Toole's guts fell out in a fountain of blood and fluid. His scream rose in pitch to a shriek, then a hideous wail. Frantically he dropped his useless Bowie and tried with both hands to stuff his intestines back inside the now hollow cavity of his abdomen. All the while he worked he grew weaker, sagging to his knees, entrails slipping through his gore-smeared fingers, to plop on the dusty ground time after time. His screech faded out and he uttered a deep, soulful moan. Piteously he raised haunted eyes to Rebecca's implacable face.

"Why? Why you done th-this to me?"

"For all those little girls and boys, you lard-gutted piece of shit," she told him coldly. "For Sue Ann Marshal. For my mother and for me. Now you can burn in hell for all eternity."

Bobby O'Toole gulped in a deep draught of air,

threw back his head and shrieked with the power of the Furies. "Whyyyyyyy meeeeeee!"

Then he shuddered mightily, groaned and fell over in the sticky pool of his own body juices.

"God! That was . . . that was sickening, Rebecca," Lone Wolf managed to force out in a gulp.

"So was he. Now we go after the others."

Two townsmen trotted up along with Tom Allison. Tom spoke for them. "We heard about Matt. Sorry. But he'll be all right. Doc Silver will fix him up good as new. The gang has pulled out, what's left of them. I saw Tulley and Styles at the head of them, makin' tracks down the road to Wyoming."

"Again! They've escaped me again?"

"Looks that way. All except Flora Belle Chase. She's at the Mother Lode," Tom told her.

"Let's find your horse and mine and ride after the gang," Lone Wolf urged.

A wicked glint came into Rebecca's eyes. "No. They can come later. Right now I want a little talk with Flora Belle. Yes. I want very much to see her."

TWENTY

Not everyone had deserted Flora Belle. While she frantically packed, and her "regular" girls made ready for flight, four gunmen waited downstairs to stave off any threat to her escape. When they saw figures with grim, set features approaching from both ends of the street, several suggested a hasty retreat.

"You do, you gotta go through me," Long Tom Wheeler growled. "Tulley, Styles and Ezekial lit outta here so fast they left most of the loot behind. I intend to get well paid for this job. Any of you have objections to splitting the take from this establishment?"

Three heads shook in negative response, the men's eyes alight with greed. Wheeler went on. "Slim, you're the best hand with powder. Suppose you go find some dynamite and let's open that safe in the office. While you're at it, we'll hold off these townies. The minute we get our hands on the gold, we haul out of here, richer and a whole lot wiser."

"What about the girls?" Sam Colter inquired.

"Hell, those fellers won't hang women. Flora Belle and her chippies will be free as birds to leave here."

"Then, let's get to doin' it," Sam enthused.

Two bullets blasted through an already shattered window and the men dove for cover. A woman's voice called from outside.

"Come out and surrender and you won't be harmed. Roger Styles and the Tulley gang got away.

They're the ones we're after. You can ride out if you give up now."

"Lordy, she's a cool one," Slim observed.

"That she is," Wheeler agreed. "Get on your way for the dynamite before they decide to put someone in the alley."

Slim hurried toward the rear entrance and two more shots sent bullets to smash bottles on the backbar.

"Time's running out," Rebecca called to them. "I want to have a little talk with Flora Belle. The rest of you can go."

"What do you think?" Sam asked Wheeler.

"Not without the money."

Sam sighed heavily. Another second passed.

Then the waiting gunslingers got their dynamite in a way they hadn't expected.

A sizzling bundle flew in through the vacant bay window, a thin trail of smoke and sparks trailing from the tip of the fuse.

"Look ou . . . !" Sam had time to shout before the explosive went off.

Much of the front of the Mother Lode bulged outward and landed in the street, shattered into kindling. The few remaining windows disintegrated. Dust and smoke billowed and swirled in the rising breeze. When the violent roar subsided, a few flames could be heard crackling inside the battered building. The frame structure moaned and creaked and the high peak roof canted forward toward the ground. From the second story came the terrified cries of the soiled doves.

"He-he, that'll learn 'em," Hard Rock Mike chortled. "Want me to give 'em another charge, Rebeckie?"

"No. I want Flora Belle alive when I get to her. I'm

going in," she announced suddenly.

"Alone?" Lone Wolf queried.

"Why not?"

Rebecca had reloaded her .44 and held it competently in her right hand as she progressed across the litter toward the sagging entrance of the Mother Lode. She stumbled slightly when her weight made a portion of the smashed plankwalk give way. Her well-honed reflexes quickly righted her and she went through the gaping hole where the batwing doors had once been.

Inside, dust fogged the large main room. She dimly saw scattered figures, lying in the grotesque postures of death. To her left a man moaned and tried to sit up. Blood ran from his ears and nose, his face had been blackened by the blast and all but his boots and pistol belt blown from his body. He raised a shaky arm to his face and wiped away the crimson flow.

"Hel . . . help me," he gasped before he fell across a table in merciful unconsciousness.

Rebecca started toward the staircase, that now hung precariously by its upper pinnings, the lower five treads blown away, along with the newel posts and bottom supports. A sudden clatter to the right and behind brought her around, the .44 American leading the way.

Long Tom Wheeler, his clothes hanging in shreds, face grimed, blood running from one ear and his nose, stood facing her now, a long-barreled Remington in his hand. A thick sliver of wood protruded from the loose flesh along his ribcage.

"You're Rebecca Caldwell. I think I liked you better as Yvette."

Wheeler started to bring his revolver into line. Rebecca had only to squeeze the trigger on the big Smith and Wesson.

Her slug caught Long Tom Wheeler in the center of his sternum. Its powerful force shoved him backward and his Remington discharged into the ceiling. An expression of curious concern crossed his face and he tried to ear back the hammer a second time. Rebecca had already cocked her weapon and wasted no time in letting the firing pin drop on a fresh cartridge.

The report sounded loud and flat in the damaged building. Rebecca's bullet traveled the short distance to Wheeler's chest and punched through a bag of Bull Durham on its way to his heart.

Tom Wheeler turned slightly, his rugged, nearly handsome features going slack, and the six-gun dropped from lax fingers. He sighed wearily, as though the world had become boresome, then collapsed in a heap among the shattered furniture. Rebecca turned away and started toward the staircase.

The treads swayed dizzily and a mighty groan came from the stair frame. Rebecca took the first flight on light, hurrying feet. She paused a moment on the landing, not looking back at the wavering run behind her. Rebecca took a deep breath, steeled herself for the risky ascent and went on.

She saw no one in the upper hallway. With the silent tread of a stalking panther, she eased along the hall. Excited voices came from several rooms, the soiled doves packing in haste and fear. She willed herself to ignore them. She had only one target.

Ahead lay the door to Flora Belle Chase's luxurious suite. Rebecca reached it and paused.

Slowly she turned the latch, her hand on the white ceramic knob. The well-oiled hinges did not betray her when she swung the door open.

A quick look showed the office-sitting room in wild disarray. Rebecca stuck her head in further and saw no sign of the woman she sought. The sound of the heavy lid of a portmanteau being closed drew her attention to the bedroom beyond. Stealthily she walked to the doorway.

"Hello, Flora Belle, *dearie*," Rebecca began in a cutting tone. "I've come to have a reckoning with you."

At the first words, Flora Belle whirled about startled and frightened. She looked at the powder grimed saloon costume that Rebecca wore, her long silken black hair in braids, bound with beaded strips of deer hide, the utilitarian cartridge belt around the girl's waist and the large revolver held competently in her small hand. The madam's mouth worked, but no sound came.

Rebecca's left hand and arm came up across her face, then hurtled out in a vicious backhand slap that knocked Flora Belle asprawl across her bed. "You fed opium to me—and to how many hundreds of other girls?—and called it candy. Poison that you dispensed as casually as bon-bons. Used to enslave us. To turn us into obedient women of no virtue, prostitutes." The anger suddenly left Rebecca to be replaced by cold deadly determination.

Flora Belle read the change in the girl who towered over her. Her hand went toward the pillows, where she kept the compact little Baby Russian taken from Rebecca. An ear-shattering report sounded and Flora Belle felt a hammer blow strike the back of her hand. Then she saw the bullet hole in the pillowcase.

She withdrew her hand, her face twisted in agony and saw the .44 sized puncture that went through both sides. Blood spurted freely and she became deathly pale. "Y-you shot me . . ." she stammered in shock.

"You intended to do me the same favor," Rebecca

returned icily. "I'd like to have you out near an ant hill. I'd stake you over it, smear your ears, nose, mouth, eyes, your nipples and your private parts with honey. That would be fitting for what you did to Sue Ann Marshal." Rebecca watched the horror that stole over the older woman. Flora Belle quaked with terror. For a moment, Rebecca's feminine compassion pleaded with her to relent. She didn't, in fact, enjoy tormenting this degenerate creature, yet vengeance must be served. She tightened her lips into a thin, hard line and bolstered her resolve.

"I got Bobby O'Toole. You might call it poetic justice, considering his . . . ah, tastes."

Compelled to know, but terrified of the answer, Flora Belle asked. "What did you do?"

"I cut his belly open. Spilled his guts out in a dirty, trash-filled alley."

A green tinge appeared around Flora Belle's mouth. She trembled in outrage and fear. "You're a monster!"

"I," A bitter laugh escaped from Rebecca's lips. *"I'm a monster?* What about Jake Tulley and my precious Uncle Ezekial giving me to the Sioux? What about you? Fondling the bodies of girls you have turned into vegetables with your opium pills and handing a twelve year old child over to the likes of Bobby O'Toole can hardly be described as humanitarian," Rebecca stormed on, her words heavily laden with sarcasm.

"But . . . I . . . I was only doing my job."

"So were Torquemada and the Holy Brothers of the Inquisition."

Flora Belle held her wrist tightly in an attempt to stem the flow of blood. Awkwardly, then, she slid off of the bed and knelt before Rebecca.

"You're not . . . not going to kill me, then, are you?"

Rebecca studied her in silence. Her mind warred with itself and she once more floundered in revulsion. As on that horrible day when Flora Belle Chase had initiated her degradation, she felt used and dirty. Tears began to run down the older woman's face and she raised quaking hands in supplication to Rebecca. Sue Ann's screams echoed in Rebecca's brain. She placed the muzzle of the .44 American against Flora Belle's forehead. The terrified lesbian quailed away from her.

"Yes, Flora Belle, I am."

Rebecca's shot sounded painfully loud in the confined room.

"I found my clothes in Flora Belle's closet," Rebecca told Lone Wolf and Hard Rock Mike half an hour later. "She had my revolver under her pillow. So I have everything back that I came here with."

"Including your honor," Lone Wolf declared.

"Yes." Rebecca thought of Flora Belle's dead face, her shattered skull with the smoking hole between her glazed eyes. "But at what price?"

"You'll be leaving now?" Mike inquired to break the awkward moment.

"We have to get after Roger Styles and the Tulley bunch," Rebecca acknowledged. "They have half a day headway on us."

Kathlene O'Day came up, her arms loaded with a large tablecloth filled with trail-hardy food. "Yer determined to carry this thing on, are you?"

"I must, Kathlene. I . . . For so long a time it's all that kept me sane in the Oglala camp. They have to be made to pay. No matter the law, the courts, or what white society thinks, I'm the one most suited to do that." Rebecca paused a moment, looked at all of